LOW DOWN DIRTY VOTE

A CRIME FICTION ANTHOLOGY
EDITED BY MYSTI BERRY

D0958513

Berry Content Corporation

Berry Content Corporation
3931 Alemany Blvd Suite 2003-257
San Francisco, CA 94132

ISBN: 1-7322258-1-8
ISBN-13: 978-1-7322258-1-7

TABLE OF CONTENTS

FOREWORD

Amy A. Miller

For almost 100 years, the American Civil Liberties Union has been working to protect constitutional rights. There's an ACLU presence in every state, fighting in the courts, in the legislatures and in the streets to ensure the promise of the Bill of Rights is fulfilled. Fighting voter suppression all over the nation is a key part of our mission.

Attacks on the right to vote seem to be relentless. States have passed voter ID requirements, shortened early voting periods, gerrymandered neighborhoods along racial lines, disenfranchised people with a conviction, and generally tried to limit voting. The impact of these laws means hundreds of thousands of voters either are turned away, or are discouraged from even showing up. The purpose of these laws seems clear: there is a concrete effort to change the shape of the electorate and make it more difficult for some people to fully participate in our community. More concerningly, the targets of these exclusions are low income people, young voters, and people of color.

Broad voting opportunities are good for voters of all ideological stripes, and our country is stronger when more voters participate. Voting demonstrates our connection to our community as we lift up our voices. Sadly, we're not at the place where everyone in our democracy can participate as a full citizen on an equal footing with everyone else at the ballot box.

If you've never faced a barrier to voting, it's easy to forget how important the right can feel when you don't have it. Last year, I spoke to a young transgender high school student who'd just won a full scholarship to pursue his dreams of majoring in political science and then going to law school. On the eve of his departure for college, I asked him what he was most excited about. I anticipated he might tell me how moving to a blue state or experiencing life in a big city was going to be his favorite part of the next year. He surprised me when he said with a bright light in his eyes that he couldn't wait to finally vote for the first time. "I've been watching and studying all of this from the sidelines," he said. "Now, finally, I'm going to be part of the solution."

I'm also reminded of the woman I met while observing the Pardons Board. The morning dragged on as people with an old felony conviction asked the three-member Board to restore their full citizenship rights. Pardons aren't handed out very often, especially since the right to carry a gun is restored, and many applicants were turned away. One elderly African American woman was told she should wait a little longer—only nine years had passed since she'd finished her sentence and the board preferred to see people after ten years. She said, "I don't even want anything except the right to vote back so I'll make sure to come back next year." The thing is, she already was eligible to vote again. Nebraska, along with about half of the U.S., allows restoration of the vote after a conviction. Laws vary from state to state, but here in the prairies you can register to vote two years after you complete your sentence. In other words, this woman might still want a pardon—but she was already eligible to vote. I followed her out to the hall to tell her that, and she burst into tears. "You mean I could have been voting the last couple of years? I feel like I just won the lottery!"

Next time you're wondering if you have time to squeeze in stopping by the polling place or talking to a friend who tells you there's no point to even casting a vote, remember what a gift this right would seem if someone had been withholding it from you even while public policies affecting your future were being made without your participation.

All of our other civil liberties—the right to protest, the right to be free from unreasonable searches, the right to privacy, the right to equal treatment—falter if we don't have a reliable election process to replace politicians who aren't honoring our other rights. As ACLU Ambassador Lewis Black says, "Elected officials shouldn't get to choose who gets to choose elected officials."

The ACLU believes in broad ballot access, and we're fighting in states across the U.S. to protect this cornerstone of democracy. Thank you—and each of these excellent authors—for your help protecting the Constitution!

Amy A. Miller
Legal Director, ACLU of Nebraska

PREFACE

MYSTI BERRY

THIS BOOK WAS BORN IN a diner somewhere in Northern California. My husband and I had been talking about how I should probably spend less time ranting on Twitter, and it got me thinking. When I was a child, voting seemed to be such a simple thing. If you were born here, or naturalized (and at eight years old, I wasn't sure what that meant), then you got to vote in every election.

Of course it was never that simple for people of color in the United States. Worse still, ever since the Supreme Court struck down provisions of the Voting Rights Act, we have been undoing much of the good that the Act required of us. With gerrymandering, repressive Voter ID laws and more, by early 2017 voting didn't feel that simple. And ranting on Twitter wasn't moving the needle at all.

In the diner that day, I pushed my diet soda glass around in its condensation puddle, feeling sad and frustrated about the overall *tarnish* that seemed to have crept over one of my favorite civic duties. In that moment a title came to me, unbidden: *Low Down Dirty Vote*. It didn't take long to figure out what I should do with that title. I'd create an anthology of crime stories by my favorite writers, on the theme of fighting voter suppression. Fund-raising felt like a much better use of my time than ranting on Twitter.

As usual, my biggest problem was confidence. The ego required to believe my stories would be interesting to the world has never felt natural to me. To complete this project, could I now double down in the ego department? Could I corral a fistful of talented crime writers? Beg, borrow, or plead my way into busy writing schedules? Would imaginations be inspired by a theme as odd as fighting voter suppression? My husband pointed out that the worst-case scenario was just people saying "no," so I said "yes."

My darling, adorable writer friends did not say no, not many of them. After my first few queries, I knew the signs that preceded a 'yes': a sudden intake of breath, eyes staring into the distance as imagination took over, and a quick "yes! And I know just what I want to write!" Even the writers who didn't have any room in their schedules made time to give me great advice and encouragement. The crime writing community is generous, and, it turns out, a huge fan of democracy.

Tom Hanks once said that doing voice-over work is harder than acting, because you have to do everything you usually do with your whole body using only your voice. He described the work as standing on your toes for twelve hours a day, reaching for the perfect performance. As I read these stories for the first time, I felt each writer stretching up on their toes. Some stories experiment with voice, others with point of view. Some have even stretched the very form of storytelling to its logical limits. Now that the day has come to share theses stories, I hope you feel as enriched as I have felt.

The miracle of the title popping into my head still puzzles me. Usually I have a tin ear for titles. However, this book's title is strong. It captures the dilemmas we face, and the sense of humor we can apply to fixing what's broke. Maybe it was on its way to Dave Eggers or Laurie R. King, but was lost and popped into my head by accident? However it happened, I'm grateful for the inspiration.

In these stories you'll travel from California to Edinburgh, as you pass through three centuries and crime fiction sub-genres from cozy to noir. An added bonus: 2018 is the hundredth anniversary of women getting the vote in the United Kingdom, and the stories in this book illustrate the struggle of women and men of all races to claim their right to vote. I'm glad we can celebrate with our friends across the pond on this important anniversary.

100% of the proceeds are being donated to the ACLU Foundation to help fight voter suppression, starting with a $5,000 advance to the ACLU against sales of this book. I hope you will be as entertained as I have been, and that one of the stories inspires you to do more than rant on Twitter, just as the title inspired me to publish this collection.

When we vote, and especially when we defend everyone's right to vote, we are powerful. We help "bend the arc of history toward justice." See you at the voting booth!

Beached

Ray Daniel

THE DESICCATED CODFISH LAY ON the smooth wet sand, disturbed only by the outline of a dog's back where Noodles had rolled on it. She looked up at me, her happy expression saying *I smell good now!*

"It's a bath for you, moron," I told the dog.

Noodles pranced about, apparently believing that the wonderful codfish odor wafting over both of us was worth any bath--goofy dog.

"How can I stay mad at you?" I asked her.

I fed her a treat then continued my run down the early-morning beach. A woman ran toward me. I gave a glance to her red hair, trim body, and toned legs then deadened my face, staring straight ahead so as not to make her nervous.

As we passed, I nodded a curt hello.

She stopped running and pointed. "What's your dog's name?"

Noodle trotted over to her. She put her hand down, giving Noodles the back to sniff.

The woman knows dogs.

I said, "Noodles. No don't do that!" She had reached down to pat him. She pulled her hand back.

"Does he bite?"

"She just rolled in a codfish."

The woman had pulled her red hair into a ponytail, framing a fair face and hazel eyes offset by a lavender running top that revealed a promise of cleavage. Her grey running shorts completed the outfit. She had somehow kicked up a piece of kelp that clung to her thigh.

"Do you mind if I run with you?" she asked. "I get creeped out that guys are looking at me."

"Of course," I said. "Guys are the worst, amiright?"

We ran on down the beach.

"You're new in town," I said.

"You the mayor or just the census taker?"

"Joppa's a small town," I said, "and we don't have a mayor. Just old-fashioned town-meeting anarchy."

"As long as they pass the school budget," she said.

She was a little faster runner than me, well maybe a lot faster. I got the sense she was throttling back her pace but my breath had started rasping.

"Are you okay?" she asked.

"Fine."

"We really can't run any slower," she said.

"No?"

"At that point, it's not really running. It's kind of jogging."

"Ah."

"Not much to say?"

"Not without oxygen."

"Just how I like my men. Breathless." She stuck out her hand. "I'm Lucy. Lucy Durant."

Hands on knees, I waved at myself, "Thomas Coffee."

Lucy, to her credit, avoided all name puns when I asked her if she'd like to meet for coffee. We now sat next to the fireplace in the Horseshoe Cafe after the lunch rush hour run. The Horseshoe, Joppa's only coffee shop, rested on a pier thrust into the Atlantic ocean. We sat on facing couches in front of a fireplace, our steaming drinks on a table before us.

"I'm surprised we got this spot," I said.

"Why?"

"The regular guys usually grab it."

"The regular guys?"

"Lou, Carl, Mel, and Arthur. They're here after breakfast every day, solving the world's problems."

"What are the world's problems?"

"The usual mix--kids today, iPhones, Congress, Town Meeting."

"Town Meeting?"

"They wouldn't miss it. They've got their own little corner."

"How do you think they'll vote tonight?"

"On the school thing?"

"Yeah."

"No telling. They don't agree on much."

"My job depends on it."

"Why?"

"Because they're voting on the budget that would pay

me."

"I think it will win. The parents will be out in force."

"Great!"

"It'll be close, though."

"Great."

Mary Barton, thin and pinched, burst into the coffee shop tugging behind her a golden retriever who seemed to have a problem with thresholds. He balked, staring at the thin strip of aluminum as if it were a steel trap. Mary's gold necklace and diamond earrings twinkled in the morning light. She dragged the dog over the threshold and approached us.

"Have you seen my father?" she asked.

"Hi Mary," I said.

"Hi. Have you seen my father?"

"This is Lucy," I said pointing.

Lucy stuck out her hand, "Lucy Durant."

Mary ignored the hand, looking around the coffee shop instead.

"He's always here," Mary said. "With his idiot friends."

"No idiots today," I said.

"I imagine they'll be back soon," Lucy said. "Town Meeting is tonight."

"Oh is that tonight?" Mary asked. "I wouldn't know. I don't own a television."

"Of course you don't," Lucy said.

"What?"

"Clearly you're too *busy* for a television."

"Well yes," Mary said tugging on the dog. "Sit, Buster! Sit!"

Buster did not sit. Instead he stuck his nose into Lucy's lap. Lucy pushed him away.

"Can you find my father, Thomas?" Mary asked me.

"You're a detective or something."

"A private investigator."

"Right. Can you find him?"

"Why not ask Roy? He's the police."

"I already have."

"And?"

"Roy is an idiot."

"I see."

"He says my dad is not officially missing."

"It's been what, three hours?"

"That's what Roy said! Can you find him? I'm worried."

I had no interest in finding Arthur for Mary. He was an irascible coot with a penchant for conspiracy theories. She was a meddlesome busybody with delusions of sophistication. The whole thing would be as much fun as a Planning Board meeting.

"I don't have time to find Arthur," I said.

"But it's your *job*."

"I get paid to do my job."

"I'll pay you," Mary said as the dog lurched away from her, trying to reach a scrid of cookie on the floor. "Goddammit, Buster, sit *down!*" She tugged the dog into submission. "How much?"

I gave her my I-really-don't-want-to-do-this rate. "Five hundred dollars a day plus expenses."

"Fine!"

"In advance."

"One sec." Mary pulled out her smartphone, poked at it. Mine dinged. My PayPal account had increased by five hundred dollars.

"I assume you've checked his apartment," I said.

"I'm too busy. That's why I just paid you five hundred dollars."

I stood, said to Lucy, "Sorry, got to go. Duty calls."

While the school budget vote was a big deal, it paled in comparison to the Great Waterfront Debate in which those who wanted to leave Joppa's waterfront in its pristine antediluvian purity battled those who thought it might be nice to erect a building or two, you know, for people.

The building folks won the town meeting vote when the builders generously, some said cynically, agreed to create a senior living apartment building, Joppa Heights, where those over sixty could abide, enjoying stunning views of the ocean without being disturbed by the youthful exuberance of forty-somethings. Arthur and his coffee cabal lived there, a short walk from the Horseshoe Cafe.

Mary Barton had taken time from her busy day to text me her father's address and I had knocked on Arthur's door. No answer. That meant little in the middle of the day. I took the elevator to the rooftop terrace where the over-sixty crowd enjoyed a swimming pool, a garden, and a big screen television that currently played a rerun Red Sox game to an empty set of seats.

A woman lay on a chaise lounge by the pool, sunning herself in a bikini--Mrs. Nash, my high school math teacher. The southern belle Mrs. Nash had looked pretty good to fifteen-year old me and she looked pretty good today as I approached the pool.

"Hi Mrs. Nash," I said.

"You can call me Alexandria now, Thomas," she said. "You're a high school graduate."

"I always think of you as Mrs. Nash."

"Well, dear, snap out of it. I divorced my husband and then outlived him."

"Good point, Alexandria."

"Or Alex if you like."

"I think I'll stick with Alexandria."

"Can I help you with something?"

"I'm looking for Arthur Krebs. His daughter Mary is worried about him."

"She'd be quite the busybody if she weren't so lazy," Alexandria said. "Bless her heart."

"Any idea where he is?"

"He did say something about shopping. Which is odd for him."

"Why?"

"He's a man."

"Are you saying that men don't go shopping?"

"I'm saying that men rarely talk about it as an activity."

"When was the last time you saw Arthur?"

"This morning."

"At breakfast?"

She fixed me with a stare. "No."

"Oh."

A breeze rustled the garden's ornamental grass. A seagull swooped overhead, cawing. A motor boat churned on the water.

"So...um...You think he's out shopping."

Alexandria stood in her bikini, walked over to the edge of the pool. "Perhaps. If he did go shopping, he's not alone."

"Why do you say that?"

"Look around. Nobody's here. They all left."

"But not you."

"I slept in."

She dove into the pool, her gray ponytail trailing behind her, with hardly a splash.

* * *

I left Alexandria Nash swimming laps and took the elevator to the apartments, then I walked down the hallways listening for televisions. A building full of people whose hearing may be going usually has at least one television blasting the latest from Fox News, but not today. Today silence reigned on floor after floor as I descended to the ground level.

Nobody home.

But that didn't necessarily mean anything. The weather was perfect, eighty-five degrees, moderate humidity, a blue sky interrupted only by jet contrails. People in Joppa, Massachusetts saw about ten of these days a year and did not waste them. Which made the shopping question even more confusing. Who would go shopping on a day like today, and why?

The elderly of Joppa congregated in three places: Joppa Heights, the Horseshoe Cafe, or the Joppa Public Library. I'd checked the first two, onward to the library.

In 1903 the Joppa Town Meeting accepted, by a vote of 128 to 126, a twenty-thousand dollar library grant from Andrew Carnegie. The close vote showed that the only thing flinty New Englanders trusted less than outsiders was money from outsiders.

I climbed the building's old granite steps, pulled open the wooden door, and stepped into the hand-rubbed oak luxury of the Gilded Age. An older woman sat at a reading table near a brick fireplace. Above the fireplace a heat exchanger blew cool air. She turned the pages of a magazine with one hand, and held her head with the other, looking for all the world like a kid who'd been left out of a game of kickball.

She looked up and saw me. "Thomas," she said. "Thomas Coffee."

Ethel Berman's son Eddie had been my best friend

growing up. Eddie lived in California now and Ethel hung out in the library.

"You look sad, Ethel."

Ethel pouted. "I miss my Eddie."

"Well, I'm sure Eddie is happy to be in his mother's thoughts."

"I need him to give me a ride to the mall."

"Oh."

"I missed the bus."

Ethel looked as if she might cry.

"The bus?"

"The shopping bus."

"What shopping bus?"

Ethel hefted a large purse onto the table and rummaged through it. She pulled out a golden gift card. The card said *$100 Joppa Heights Dollars.* "They're only good for today at the mall."

I took the card, "Where did you get this?"

"Yesterday everyone at Joppa Heights got them in the mailboxes," Edith said. "I think it's the management company trying to make up for the unheated pool."

"And there was a bus?"

"Yes, a luxury bus! It was going to take us to the mall and then to the beach."

"And you missed it."

"I forgot my gift card and had to run back upstairs. When I came back they had all left."

"Well that's a shame."

"You'd think one of them would have said something," Ethel said shaking her head. "But the bus was full. They probably didn't notice."

"Well thank you Eth—"

"Thomas, could you give me a ride to the mall?"

"I'd love to Ethel, but I'm on the clock."

"Well, I guess I'll just sit here alone."

Ethel had maneuvered me into a guilt checkmate. There was nothing to say that didn't make me look like a horrible young man. So I just ducked my head, shrugged, and backed out slowly.

I needed to see a guy about a bus.

Joppa, like many New England towns, has a hate/love relationship with tourists--it hates the tourists but loves their money. The result is a patchwork of regulations and ordinances that essentially say *Welcome to Joppa. Don't Touch Anything.*

The tourist buses are a case in point. Inspired by Boston's success with amphibious duck boats, Town Meeting narrowly passed a bylaw allowing a duck boat to drive on the streets of Joppa. The opponents of the measure had the upper hand until it was pointed out that a duck boat had already been operating in Joppa for three years and it seemed a shame to mothball it. Debate ended and the question was moved just after someone had delivered the traditional final argument. *Who will think of the children?*

The Joppa duck boat trundled through town touring the spots where ships had once been built, fish had once been caught, and slaves had once been traded. Then it entered the sea and toured the spots where ships had once been built, fish had once been caught, and slaves had once been traded. After that it brought the tourists to Gift Shop Island, an island containing only one structure and no entertainment.

Jake Stern owned the duck boat company. Since he was capped at one duck boat, he'd recently invested his vast duck boat earnings into a luxury tour bus that would take people down to Boston in style. It was the only bus in town, and so I headed over to Jake's garage where I found Jake, bald and fat, sitting in an empty garage typing furiously.

"What an asshole!" Jake said.

I glanced at his screen. "You have got to get off Facebook."

"I'm not on it that much."

I nudged him aside, clicked the mouse on the discussion. "There's 232 comments here."

"There are no fucking fish!"

"This again, Jake?"

"This guy wants his kid to be a fisherman!"

"I know."

"But there are no fucking fish! It's just logic."

"Well, I'm sure you've convinced him."

Jake reached around me for the keyboard.

I blocked him. "Can I ask you a quick question?"

"What."

"Where's your bus?"

He looked up as if he'd been teleported into his own garage. Looked around, then at me.

"I don't see how that's your business, Thomas."

"I'm just looking for Arthur Krebs. I think he's on a bus."

"Not my problem. Have you asked Mary?"

"Mary hired me."

"That woman's got too damn much money."

"So where's the bus?"

Jake stood, headed for the rest room. I followed him in. He stood in front of a urinal, worked it.

"Jesus, can you give a guy some privacy?" Jake asked.

"I just need to know where the bus is."

"No idea," said Jake, turning and leaving the bathroom without a glance at the sink. I washed my hands out of pure OCD habit and followed him out. Jake was already back at his computer.

"Shithead!" Jake yelled at the screen.

"You going to Town Meeting tonight?" I asked.

"And vote on the special school budget? I don't care what they do."

"Because, you know, I thought you might want to comment when I speak."

"Yeah, I heard you were seeing one of the new teachers."

"I'm not *seeing* her. We had coffee this morning."

"Not what I heard."

What happens in the Horseshoe Cafe, clearly doesn't stay in the Horseshoe Cafe.

"Well, I wasn't planning to talk about the school budget. I was planning to talk Boston's duck boats."

Jake could be an asshole, but he was a smart asshole. He turned from the screen, stood.

"Yeah? What about Boston's duck boats?"

"Well, you know they changed their duck boat rule. Now they need a driver *and* a tour guide. Driver can't do both."

"That's because they're driving in Boston traffic. We've got no Boston traffic here!"

"Don't you think that Town Meeting should know about the new rule?"

"No!" Jake said stepping toward me. "I do *not* think they should know about the new rule. I can't afford two people on the duck boat."

I didn't back away. "Well, given that we don't even know where your bus is—"

"Oh for fuck's sake. Rusty has it!"

"What's he doing with it?"

"He got some freelance gig and we're splitting the money."

"Who paid him?"

"I don't have to tell you that."

I turned to leave. "I understand. We'll probably find out where Arthur and the rest are at Town Meeting. I can ask them about the duck boat question too."

Jake dropped himself back into his desk chair, glanced at the screen. "Oh for God's sake. Jessica Crystal hired the bus."

"Thanks, Jake," I said.

"So you're not going to bring up that Boston thing at Town Meeting?"

"Me?" I said, walking out the door. "Why would I go to Town Meeting?"

While the Joppa website will tell you that we are "nestled by the sea," it will not tell you to visit our beaches. That's because we have only one beach and it's crap, good only for running. The federal government created Greenhead Beach (the official name is Joppa Beach, but nobody calls it that) by dumping tons of gritty brown sand in a cove. I knew Jessica Crystal would be there, overseeing her son's swimming lessons along with the other moms.

Jessica Crystal had the long, lithe body of a rich mom. She stood on the beach in her white bikini, shielding her eyes from the sun with one hand as a breeze stirred her long black hair. She and her husband were the town's version of a power couple. He bought companies, then turned them around and sold them for what must have been tremendous profit. She presided over the PTO.

Their ten-year-old son, Trevor, stood in waist-deep water,

wearing a life preserver. A cowled hat shaded his neck. His slathering of sunscreen had created a tiny oil-soaked Superfund site in the water around him. The instructor had the kids dunking their face in the water and blowing bubbles.

"Don't breathe the water, baby!" Jessica called.

"God, I hated those swimming lessons," I said. "My mom made me do them."

Jessica startled. Gave me a stern look. "Thomas, it's impolite to sneak up on people."

"Sorry I—"

"I am *trying* to keep my son safe."

"Trevor's wearing a life jacket."

"Did you know that it's possible to drown in two inches of water?"

"If you're a vole," I muttered.

"What?"

"Also that girl standing next to him is a lifeguard."

"Is there something I can help you with?" Jessica asked, staring at her son's bubble-blowing.

"I'm looking for Arthur Krebs."

"Mary's father?"

"She hired me."

"He is a horrible man."

"Well, I'll admit that he—"

"Did you know that he voted for Trump?"

"It happens. Anyway, he's missing along with most of the people from Joppa Heights."

Jessica waved at the water. "Trevor, honey, check your fingertips! Don't get pruney!"

Trevor ignored her.

Good for him!

"Jake Stern said that you hired a bus from Rusty."

"Well, *we* hired a bus."

"Who's we?"

"The PTO. We wanted to do something nice for the elderly."

"Even the Trump-voting elderly?"

Jessica stopped staring at the water, gave me a high wattage smile. "You know. Kill them with kindness."

"Mary doesn't seem to see it as a kindness."

"Mary doesn't have a son in the school system."

"So where did Rusty—"

"Oh thank God it's over," Jessica said. Trevor was tromping out of the water with the rest of the group. "Goodbye, Thomas, I have to go be a parent."

She walked off in her white bikini, waving at Trevor because apparently he would be unable to find her without help, though she was really quite hard to miss.

Mary Barton had paid me five hundred dollars plus expenses to find her father. This made two things clear. One was that I'd have to go to the mall to find him, and second that "plus expenses" could easily include a late lunch with Lucy at said mall.

"Mall lunch," Lucy said, sitting in my car. "Thomas, you do know how to treat a girl."

"The best for you. We'll walk right past that food court and go to a place with napkins on every table."

"On *every* table? Where would I see such a wonder?"

"The Rain Forest Cafe."

"Oh my…"

We pulled into the parking lot. "But first I have to find the bus."

We circled the lot.

"Where would you park a bus?" Lucy asked. "And why

27

would you give a shopping trip to the elderly."

"You mean beyond killing them with kindness?"

"Let's assume that wasn't the real reason."

We drove around the back of the mall, looking for a bus lot. No buses, but not a surprise. In a region full of tourist attractions, the Cherry Hill Mall with its Target and Rain Forest Cafe was not a likely place to find a busload of tourists.

"I think the real reason is to keep them away from Town Meeting," I said. "Tip the vote."

"But how long can they stay at the mall?" Lucy asked.

Good Question.

We drove around and found no bus. They hadn't stayed at the mall. Ethel had said something about a beach.

"We'd better get back to town," I said. "Maybe Jessica will know where they went to the beach."

"There goes my chance to use a table napkin," Lucy said.

I have a daily challenge with lunch. The question is whether to eat lunch when I'm hungry, usually at eleven o'clock in the morning, or stick with convention and save my lunch until noon. I haven't made it to noon in forty-seven consecutive days.

Today, I'd missed lunch all together. Lucy too had missed lunch and now we were both stuck in traffic and hangry.

"What could possibly be causing this traffic?" Lucy asked.

"Beach," I said.

"The friggin' beach? I thought the town had a beach."

"Well, it's more of a 'beach'," I said making air quotes. "Everyone who wants to go to a real beach heads over to the next town, Abenaki. They have three beaches there, all

28

natural."

"So why the traffic?"

"The tourists all go to the beach at the same time and all come home at the same time. It's five o'clock. Their kids are hungry."

"So are their girlfriends."

"We had coffee together. Now you're my girlfriend?"

"Not anymore. I'm starving."

"Well that was a short-lived romance."

"For want of a taco…"

We inched our way off the highway.

"I'll make it up to you," I said. "I'm flush with dough and on expenses."

"Oh yeah? How?"

"We'll head over to the Bluefish Brewery. We can sidestep the crowd, eat dinner at the bar."

"Sounds great. Does this thing have a siren?"

I pointed at the dashboard of my aging Lexus. "It doesn't even have a CD player."

Lucy crossed her arms and sulked. I edged us along, inched past the duck boat garage. Saw the bus was still missing.

"Of course it's still missing," Lucy said. "Town Meeting is at seven."

"I just had to check."

"So hungry…"

I finally got downtown and parked. The sidewalks had filled with tourists wearing newly bought Joppa gear, T-shirts, and lobster hats from Gift Shop Island. We weaved between them to the Bluefish Brewery, stepped past the line at the hostess station, and found two seats at the bar.

We also found Rusty Ash, the bus driver.

"Jesus, Rusty, what are you doing here?" I asked.

"I'm having supper," answered Rusty with a slushy *s*.

"What's for supper?" Lucy asked pointing at a shot glass. "Whiskey with a beer chaser?"

"It's rye!"

"You're shit-faced!" I said.

"I don't have a drinking problem!" Rusty said.

"I didn't say you had a drinking problem," I said.

Jesus, this guy has a drinking problem.

"Where's the bus?"

"What?"

"The bus. The bus full of old people."

"That's not my fault! They made me leave?"

"Who's they?"

"The PTO. Jessica picked me up, gave me a hundred dollar tip and dropped me here."

"Where are they?"

"Pogie Beach in Abenaki."

"Aw shit. I gotta go," I told Lucy.

"Just call the cops," Lucy said.

"The cops in Abenaki? They're useless."

"You got that right, brother," Rusty said raising his beer. "Snooty bastards."

"I took Mary's money and said I'd find Arthur. So I'm going to find Arthur."

Lucy slumped onto a bar stool next to Rusty, who looked her up and down. "Whatever. I'll just eat here."

I caught Meg the bartender's attention, handed her a credit card.

"Meg, I'm covering Lucy's dinner," I said.

"I'll cover my own dinner, thank you," Lucy said.

"It's the least I can do."

"That's for sure."

"I gotta go," I said and turned to leave.

Lucy called after me. "Thomas, if you leave I won't be here when you get back."

"Of course you won't," I said as I walked out the door. "How long does it take to eat dinner?"

Talk about stating the obvious.

I swung by my house and picked up Noodles, who needed a long walk, and swung by the garage and picked up Jake Stern who needed a Facebook intervention. Jake was now the town's only sober bus driver.

I'd thought that getting Jake away from his computer would have freed him from Facebook's hold, but he simply switched to his cell phone. Jake spent the ride fighting with a Steelers fan about whether the Patriots were cheaters and whether Tom Brady was the Greatest Of All Time. He'd argued, swore, and ignored me until we lost cell service. I'd have talked to Noodles but she was sleeping.

We parked, climbed out of the car. Noodles ran into the dunes to find something to roll in. Jake and I walked on toward the bus.

Despite the perfect weather, the beautiful scenery, and the comfort of a fully stocked luxury tour bus, it became apparent that things had gotten ugly.

Lord of the Flies ugly.

The bus's luggage panels had been opened. Inside sat a blue cooler behind two older women wearing summer dresses and stern expressions.

"That's rationed, young man," said one of the women.

"Rationed? You rationed the water?"

"We didn't know how long we'd be here. People were drinking us dry."

"So you took it on yourself to ration the water?"

"It *had* to be done!"

I flipped open a cooler filled with water and ice. "Nobody's drunk any."

"Each person gets two per day."

Jake said, "How long did you think you'd be here?"

"Who are you?"

"The bus driver," Jake said climbing aboard the bus. "What the hell happened in here? And what's that smell?"

I left Jake and the water guardians behind, walked down wooden steps to the beach where another group of ladies sat on the sand.

"Ladies, the bus driver is here," I said.

"Well," said a woman with short-cropped grey hair, jeans, and a tank top. "I am *not* going to ride in a bus with those bitches."

"There's only one bus."

"They can *walk!*"

"Where are all the men?" I asked.

"Dead."

"They don't live as long as women," said another lady.

"I mean the ones who came to the beach with you."

"Oh."

She pointed. Several men stood on a sand dune watching one wave a cell phone around. I climbed the dune. There stood Lou, Carl, and Mel. No Arthur. I climbed the dune and joined them.

"Still no signal," Carl said. "How can there be no signal?"

"I told you there'd be no signal," answered Lou.

"I thought maybe when the sun went lower."

"No, that's AM radio. Lou said, "There's no signal because *you two* voted against the cell tower!"

"It's not our fault."

"It lost by one vote."

"I voted against it because cell towers cause cancer," Carl said.

"They *don't* cause cancer, you idiot. They cause phone coverage."

"If they don't cause cancer then when why are they called cell towers?"

"What?"

"Because of the cells!"

Mel said, "Also they're ugly."

"Oh for Christ's—"

"Have any of you seen Arthur?"

"He's gone," Mel said.

"Gone?" Lou asked, looking around. "What did he do? Get a ride home with a random family?"

Carl said, "That's what I should have done." He shook his phone. "There's still no phone service here."

Mel said, "He and Linda said they were walking back."

"Ha. Linda. I'd like to walk *her* back," Carl said.

"Keep it clean," Lou said.

"So he's walking? He'll miss the bus."

"What bus?"

"I brought the bus driver. You're saved."

"I *told* you two that prayer would work better than a cell phone," Mel said.

While Jake herded the remaining senior citizens onto his bus, I called Noodles to go looking for Arthur. The dog didn't respond. She had disappeared into the beach grasses. She was probably eating something that would give her a tapeworm or diarrhea, or both.

I walked out of the parking lot and turned up the road toward town. I was pretty sure I could catch up to Arthur and Linda, as long as they didn't hitchhi--

Noodles' barking traveled over the dune. She'd probably

found another dog. Or a rabbit. I veered off the road and climbed the dune, cresting it and saw her. Noodles barked again and pawed the ground behind a bush. I walked up to Noodles, reached for her color and heard a voice.

"Shut up, you stupid dog!" Arthur said. "Go on! Scat!"

He and Linda lay on a blanket behind the bush, hidden from everyone except Noodles.

"Ahhh!" screamed Linda reaching for her scattered bikini.

"Oh God I'm sorry!" I said averting my eyes. "Noodles get away from them! Come here!"

"Thomas, this dog is a menace!" Arthur yelled as I grabbed Noodles' collar.

"Bus leaves in five minutes," I said and fled back over the dune.

I dropped Noodles at home and met the bus at Town Hall. I really should have called Lucy to deliver a *mea culpa*, but finding out what happened at Town Meeting seemed more fun. The residents of Joppa Heights filed out of the bus, grumpy and sunburned, and headed up the steps into Town Hall. Arthur led the way. I walked next to him, the better to see.

Five hundred Town Meeting heads turned as our group entered the hall. Arthur went to the check-in table where Jessica Crystal sat wearing a red dress and wielding a red pen.

"We're here to check in," Arthur said.

"You are too late," Jessica said. "The meeting has started."

"That's bullshit."

"People cannot just walk in here—"

Peter Appleton, the town moderator, spoke from the

stage using the microphone, "Is there a problem in the back?"

Arthur called back, "Jessica is saying that we can't join the meeting because we're late."

"Jessica is wrong," Appleton said. "Take your seats so we can get this over with."

The busload of senior citizens sat, filling in the empty seats that always adorned the back of the hall.

"Now, " Appleton said. "We were—"

"Point of order!" Arthur called out.

"Yes, Arthur."

Arthur Krebs walked to the podium, tapped the microphone.

"I want it to be noted that over sixty of us were taken out to Pogie beach and *left there* so that we could not vote in this town meeting!"

"That's ridiculous, Arthur," Jessica called from the check-in table.

"It's the truth! The PTO has plotted to keep us from voting on this school budget."

"Sit down, Arthur!" said a voice from the crowd.

Moderator Appleton banged his gavel. "We *will* follow the rules of order!"

"What did you think, Jessica?" Arthur asked. "Did you think we were all going to vote against your precious school budget?"

"Of course you were!" Jessica said.

Linda, now wearing a shawl over her bathing suit, stood and pointed. "That's ageist! We don't vote as a block!"

Arthur said, "We can't agree on anything. Except we did this time."

"All of you sit down and be quiet!" Appleton said banging his gavel. "Right now!"

Arthur remained standing. "I make a motion that we move the question!"

"Seconded!" Linda called out.

Appleton rolled his eyes. "We have a motion to move the question of the school budget. All in favor." He looked out at the audience. "All opposed." He looked again. "The ayes have it. We'll vote on the question."

"That's crazy!" Jessica called. "They can't walk in and take over."

"Vote!" Appleton said. "All in favor!"

My hand went up along with some others around the room.

"All opposed!"

More hands went up. In the back rows the Joppa Heights contingent, stood and voted *No* as a block.

"The *noes* have it," Appleton said from the podium.

Jessica Crystal stormed from the room.

A week later, Lucy sat across from me in the Horseshoe finishing a cup of coffee and a scone. I'd noticed that she tended to make the coffee and the scone disappear at the same time. My scone was long gone, and I now sipped coffee.

"I still don't see why you have to leave now," I said.

"Because I'm a school teacher, Thomas, and Joppa isn't hiring school teachers."

"Spend the summer. We're good at summer."

Lucy finished her scone, then her coffee, and stood. We walked past Arthur, Carl, Lou, and Mel who had taken their usual spot by the fireplace.

"Lucy's leaving, Arthur," I said. "Thanks a *lot* guys."

"I was going to vote yes," Arthur said.

"Yeah, you would," Mel said. "They're wasting enough

money on those schools."

"Public education is immoral anyway," Carl said. "Nothing but brainwashing."

"Jesus, Carl, get off the Fox News," Lou said. "I was going to vote yes," he said to Lucy.

"Fox News has got nothing to do with—"

"Well, bye-bye, gentlemen," Lucy said. "It's been something else."

She headed for the door.

"Did she just insult us?" Arthur asked me.

I shrugged and followed her. I untied Noodles from the bike rack and walked Lucy to her packed car. She gave me a hug.

"So you're really leaving," I said.

"Yup."

"What about us?"

"We'll always have Facebook."

Lucy climbed into her car, fired it up and took off down the road.

I looked down at Noodles and then out to the beach.

"C'mon," I said. "I need a run."

Noodles ran out onto the beach, sniffing for codfish.

About Ray Daniel

Ray Daniel is an award-winning author of Boston-based crime fiction. His short story "Give Me a Dollar" won a 2014 Derringer Award for short fiction and "Driving Miss Rachel" was chosen as a 2013 distinguished short story by Otto Penzler, editor of *The Best American Mystery Stories 2013*.

Daniel's short fiction has been published in the Level Best Books anthologies *Thin Ice*, *Blood Moon*, *Stone Cold*, and *Rogue Wave*, as well as in the Anthony-nominated anthology *Murder At The Beach* (Down and Out Books).

His novels, *Terminated*, *Corrupted Memory*, *Child Not Found*, and *Hacked* have been published by Midnight Ink. *Hacked* is the fourth novel in the Tucker Mysteries. *Child Not Found* and *Hacked* have received starred reviews from *Publisher's Weekly*. *Child Not Found* has received a starred review from the *Library Journal*.

To find out more about Ray Daniel, visit http://www.raydanielmystery.com/bio/.

A CLEAN SWEEP

ANN PARKER

"NO! I TOLD YOU AFORE. It's unnatural!" Tom Johnson pointed a threatening finger at his wife. "No wife of mine is going to set foot near a ballot-box. Period. It's against the laws of God and nature."

Sarah Sue Johnson took a deep breath, trying to calm the leap of panic in her breast. Her heart was pounding so hard it was as if it would burst straight through her stays.

She had told herself she would try, one more time, to talk to Tom, since today was voting day, but she should have known it would not go well. When had such discussions ever gone well? Why did she keep thinking he would change?

"Tom, these are modern times now. It's is the year of our Lord, eighteen-hundred and seventy. This is Wyoming

Territory. Wyoming, the land of opportunity...that's what you said, when we moved here. I know you don't hold with the governor—"

Tom spat. On her clean floor.

She continued, "—But it's the law now and has been that way for nearly a year."

Tom's face just grew darker and darker. "Don't try to tell me about the law, woman. Just because it's law don't make it right."

She continued, determined to say her piece to its end, no matter what. "I'm begging you, Tom," she tried to soften her tone. "It means a lot to me. I want to be there, cast my vote, and be a part of this historical occasion."

"Hold your tongue!" His black eyed gaze snapped at her, like a spark that escaped the cooking stove, threatening to burn everything down.

He'd stopped pointing. His hand had balled into a fist and was by his side. He took a step toward her, and she took one wary step back, broom clutched in her hands, eyes on his fist with its white knuckles and repeated, "It's the law, Tom."

He sneered. "The bill was a joke that got out of hand. The legislature was just trying to put that Yankee governor in his place, embarrass him by giving him a piece of tomfoolery legislation and force him to veto it. They never figured him for signing it."

The sneer turned into a glowering frown. "I knew it was a mistake to bring those newspapers home. If you took proper care of your tasks, you'd have no time to be reading newspapers and books and thinking about things that a woman shouldn't be thinking about." His eyes swept around the kitchen, his accusing glance kicking up against the pile of newspapers sitting alongside the dirty breakfast dishes, still on the table. "Leave the politics to men, like it oughta be."

"So, a man, who works every day—and don't you tell me regular that man's work is harder than any women's work? —has time to read the newspaper every day and step round to the ballot-box once a year. But a woman doesn't? I've been doing everything you've asked, everything! And I've read the papers same as you. I've read about the candidates and what they stand for. I know my own mind."

"Your own *mind?*" Tom's voice rose on that last word, disbelieving. "You've been listening to the drivel that Mrs. Whittaker and the other local suffragists have been spewing. You just keep in mind what The Good Book says in Timothy—'Let the woman learn in silence with all subjection. I suffer not a woman to teach, nor to usurp authority over the man, but to be in silence.'"

She could never stand it when he threw Bible verse at her. And right then, she made her mistake. She opened her mouth and said: "Mr. Johnson, if the good Lord didn't want women to *teach*, then you tell me why He's allowing— in fact, I'd say *encouraging*—all these young ladies, straight out of normal school, to come on out into this wide-open wild country of the West to fill the schoolhouses and *teach* the young'uns with the approval of all you men!"

He moved so fast that Sarah had no time to retreat or react.

His open palm smacked hard against her cheekbone. Her head snapped back, sight blurred with sudden tears of pain. From what seemed a great distance, she heard the broom clatter to the plank floor as, too late, she raised her hands to protect herself.

"No more of your lip," Tom said through gritted teeth. "I've got to go open the store. All your crazy talk has made me late, and folks'll be waiting. I'm saying this only once more. If you know what's good for you, put all that voting and women's suffrage nonsense out of your mind, right now. If I hear word you went to vote on the sly, it'll be all the worse for you."

She shrank away from him until she felt the heat of the black stove crawling up her spine.

He turned away, and drew a finger along a windowsill, leaving a small cleared trail through the grit. "This place is so dusty, it's a disgrace. Clean it. And see if you can't make biscuits that aren't like to break a man's teeth when he tries to bite into them."

Without a glance at her, he walked to the front of the house, pulled his derby off the hook by the front door, and left, slamming the door so hard the frame house shook.

Sarah Sue picked up her broom and sank into the nearest kitchen chair, hand cradling her burning cheek. "If you're going to quote from The Good Book, Tom," she whispered, "what of Colossians 3:11? 'Husbands, love your wives, and do not be harsh with them.'"

Of course, he wasn't there to answer. And that was just as well, because she knew what he would do.

Besides, Sarah Sue now had made up her mind, and she wasn't going to change it. She knew exactly what she was going to do.

First, she was going to do her chores, and make sure that Tom could find no fault once he came home.

Then, she was going to change into her Sunday-best clothes, go down into the root cellar, and retrieve her hidden carpetbag that held a change of clothes, the pin money she'd saved up over the past two miserable years of marriage, and her letters from Sissy and her mother.

Next, she would go down to the train station and buy a

ticket to Cheyenne for the five-ten out of town so she could be long gone before Tom arrived home after closing up the store at six o'clock.

The last thing she would do before boarding the train would be to vote.

Her sister Sissy had been trying to get her to leave Tom, from the very start. Sissy knew what he was, what he'd been doing to Sarah. Sissy's last letter had said it plain as it could be said: *Leave him and come stay with me here in Cheyenne. The town is short of teachers, and, as you probably know, with the law passed last year, all teachers are now paid the same whether they were men or women. You will get a position as easy as snapping your fingers and make a fresh start.*

Cheek throbbing, Sarah stepped through the next hours, focused on her daily chores—washing the dishes, redding up the two bedrooms where she and Tom slept separately, sewing a button on one of Tom's shirts that she'd washed yesterday and ironing it, preparing the biscuits he claimed were hard as rocks, and dusting—*for the last time*, she told herself. Her soul rose and sang as each task was completed *for the last time*.

She even went so far as to prepare a cold dinner for Tom when he came home. Tom had his routine and would take his noontime supper at the saloon hard by while Old Joe watched the store, she was certain. She left the plate with his evening meal covered and ready, along with a carefully penned note saying good-bye, but not much more.

She saved the sweeping for last, starting at the front door and moving through the house to the mudroom and out the back door.

Finished with sweeping the rear porch, Sarah Sue paused, leaned over the broom handle and looked out for the last time over the rolling landscape, the yellowing prairie grasses, the distant mountains. The late afternoon chirrup of insects and the warmth of the sun made the September day almost feel like summer. But the snow powdering the mountain tops, and a breeze, cool and clean to the skin, served as reminders of autumn. The wind gusted, twisting her petticoats and the long skirt of her faded calico housedress about her lower limbs as if determined to hold her in place.

But nothing could make her stay now. Not the wind, not Tom and his threats and his hateful words.

Sarah took a deep breath, trying to draw inner strength from the raw and wild nature beyond her back porch.

"I'm ready," she said aloud, to none but herself. "Time to go." She pictured the railroad tracks leading out of town, the steel road to Cheyenne, where Sissy and a new life awaited.

Sarah went into her bedroom and leaned the broom against the wall as she prepared to change. Out of the worn housedress—*to never be worn again!*—and into a fresh shirtwaist, her Sunday-best checkered skirt with its matching belted jacket, her favorite bonnet, and sturdy boots for travel.

She looked at herself in the small mirror nailed to the wall. The redness where he had struck her was already turning into a bruise, but only partly noticeable beneath the bonnet's wide-ruffled brim. Once she pulled a travel veil over her face, no one would see this, the latest of the indignities and hurts that he had piled upon her.

All she needed now was the carpetbag and her cloak, and she could walk out of the house and never look back. At the last minute, she took her apron embroidered by Sissy's loving hand and given to her on her wedding day. She couldn't stand the idea that this gift of her sister's should stay behind to face whatever rage Tom might wreak upon it in her absence.

Sarah hurried to the kitchen, knelt, and slid the bolt back that led to the outsized root cellar. Tom was inordinately proud of this structure, boasting how his house was the only one in town with a cellar large enough for a man to stand up in. Not that he ever ventured down there; as a storage area for root vegetables and her home-canned goods, it was a "woman's domain."

Which made it all the easier for Sarah Sue to hide her traveling bag from his prying eyes.

She climbed down the steep ladder-like stairs from light to gloom. In the dim, dank belowground, her glass jars of sauerkraut and other preserves glimmered on the shelves, while the dried fruit dangled from the ceiling like edible decorations. The barrel of potatoes, straight from the earth, offered a dusty scent. She added the folded apron to her bag and climbed back up the steep set of ladder stairs. *Done.*

Then she remembered: her faithful broom, still leaning against the bedroom wall.

Loathe to leave a single item out of place, Sarah set her bag down and hurried into the bedroom. Just as she grabbed the broom, she heard the door slam.

A familiar, dreaded tread through the house, then:

"Sarah Sue! What the Sam Hill is going on here?"

Tom!

What was he doing home early?

Unable to believe her ears, fear surging through her, she emerged from the bedroom. There he was, standing by her carpetbag and the gaping cellar opening, arms akimbo.

Holding tight to the broom as if it were her single line to courage, Sarah knew the moment was now. She had to be brave. She had to be strong.

"You left the store?" Her words came out as an accusation.

He ducked his chin, momentarily defensive. "I closed early to vote. I thought I'd take you with me."

"You, you're going to let me vote?" Had she heard his words aright? Maybe he had listened to her, thought it over, and changed his mind. Maybe she was making a mistake...

He shrugged, dismissive. "I thought about it and realized, two votes is better'n one. It's a tight race, and I'm not about to see the party of Lincoln run roughshod over us. So, you come with me and vote like I tell you." He glanced down at the carpetbag. "Now, what's all this?"

Her wavering resolve hardened. *He hasn't changed. He'll never change.*

She said, "What this is, is I'm leaving you, Tom."

He blinked. Then, she saw in his eyes, in his face, that he understood. "The hell you are! I'll kill you first!"

His hand curled into a fist and he stepped toward her.

Panic screamed inside. Without thinking, Sarah brought the broom up and swatted him in the chest. "Stay away from me!" she shouted.

Off-balance, he staggered back, grabbing at the broom straws for balance. His foot flailed in empty air over the gaping cellar entrance. She thrust the broom at his chest hard. He fell back...and down...his tight grip ripping the broom from her hands.

A clatter, a crash, and a yowl of pain rose from the cellar.

With a strength and speed borne of fear and fury, Sarah raced to the trap door, heaved it up and over with a slam, and shot the bolt home.

She stood up and to one side. Hands smarting with splinters, she gripped the strings of her bonnet, hardly able to believe what she'd done.

Was he dead? Had she killed him?

And she realized that she didn't really care, only she certainly didn't want to hang for killing such a worm of a man and be doomed to eternal damnation. He wasn't worth it.

Muffled, but distinct, she heard the crash of glass—one of her jars of preserves, no doubt. She hoped it was the pickled pigs' feet, which always stunk to high heaven.

"Damn it, woman! Let me out of here right now!" She could hear his voice clearly, which meant he could hear hers.

She leaned over the locked trap door. "You listen to me, and you listen well, Mr. Johnson. Do you think I'm so stupid as to let you out after you threatened to kill me? No, Mr. Johnson. I'm leaving. I'm leaving now, and I'm going to vote my mind, and you'll never see nor hear from me again."

"You can't leave me here, Sarah Sue!" His anger held a touch of panic. He started pounding on the latched door, probably with the broom handle, she thought.

"Of course I can, and I will! And don't bother with your pitching a fit, because no one's going to hear you down there." Then she relented, just a little. "Tomorrow morning, when you don't show to open the store, Old Joe'll come by looking for you. Then you can start yelling and pounding."

"You can't do this, damn you!"

"You are in no position anymore to tell me what I can and cannot do, you and your blaspheming ways." She picked up her bag.

The muffled words from below came up loud and clear. "You'll be going to Hell for this, Sarah Sue!"

That did it.

She dropped her bag, walked over to stand on the trap door, and stamped hard with her sturdy travel boots, for all she was worth. There was a yelp and clatter from below.

It pleased her mightily to think what her vigorous response must have sounded like to him, down there in the pitch dark, amongst the potatoes, carrots, cabbages, dried apples, pickled onions and pigs' feet, and sauerkraut she'd put up over the summer. That thump probably thundered like the voice of God from on high.

She yelled back, "I've *been* in Hell for the past two years, Mr. Johnson, just by being your wife. And I'm done!"

And then, for good measure, even though it wasn't a Christian thing to do, she stomped on the latched cellar entrance again.

Sarah turned on her heel and walked out of the house, trembling at her own audacity and, yes, trembling in fear that somehow he'd magically escape, come running up behind her, and grab her by the throat.

By the time she reached the train station, Sarah felt calmer. Once she had her ticket in hand, she felt calmer still. *Only one more thing to do.*

The polling place was easy to find, being that it was in the building right next to the train station. She wasn't but heading in that direction when, right away, the ballot peddlers surrounded her, trying to shove their party's ballots into her hands with a "Wouldn't you be voting for the party of Lincoln, the party of franchise, ma'am?" and "Surely you'll show your appreciation to the Wyoming legislature by taking up the cause for the party brought the bill to vote." She chose the ballot with the broad red stripes on the back.

A handful of men and one woman waited for their turns

with the election judges. Sarah, glad that there were only a few folks—she had a train to catch, after all—got in line. The woman in front of her, also holding a red-striped ballot, turned around. Sarah recognized her from church: the suffragist Mrs. Whittaker. The two women greeted each other with polite smiles. Mrs. Whittaker's gaze fixed on the bruised side of Sarah Sue's face, and her smile faded. Suddenly nervous, Sarah turned her head away to hide from the woman's inspection.

But then, she realized: she had nothing to be ashamed about, unless it was that it had taken her so long to see her husband for the monster he was.

No more hiding.

Sarah Sue squared her shoulders and forced herself to look back at Mrs. Whittaker, straight on.

To her surprise, there was no censure in the other woman's expression, only a knowing compassion. Mrs. Whittaker's next words were full of calm and determined cheer. "It is a great day for women, isn't it, Mrs. Johnson. The flame of enfranchisement has been lit at last, and it will never go out. It has been a long journey of pluck and perseverance, don't you agree?"

Thinking of the ticket in her pocket, the carpetbag and ballot in one gloved hand, Sarah allowed her lips to smile, embracing the pain in her cheek. "It has been a long road, Mrs. Whittaker. But well worth it, because here we are."

Mrs. Whittaker paused, then asked, "Is...everything all right, Mrs. Johnson?"

Sarah Sue touched the bruise, her badge of courage. "Nothing to worry about, Mrs. Whittaker, just a miscalculation with the broom. And after all is said and done, I did manage to make a clean sweep."

Author's Note

On December 10, 1869, Wyoming's territorial legislators passed a bill that was signed into law granting women the right to vote. In a general election on September 6, 1870, 70-year-old Mrs. Louisa A. Swain of Laramie, Wyoming, became the first woman to cast a vote in Wyoming and, by extension, in all of the United States.

As to why Wyoming, and why then...well, there are all kinds of stories and theories. It helps in reading about this timeframe to keep in mind that, "back then," the Democrats were the conservative party, while the Republicans were more "progressive" (this is a simplistic summary, but will do for this story!). In an article "Right Choice, Wrong Reasons: Wyoming Women Win the Right to Vote" on the site WyoHistory.org, author Tom Rhea notes that when the Wyoming territorial legislature—which was controlled by the Democratic Party, met in October 1869, it passed a law guaranteeing that teachers—most of whom were women—would be paid the same whether they were men or women. They also put forth a bill to give (white) women the right to vote.

All of this was pretty radical thinking for mid-19th century. However, it seems that the Democrats might have had various reasons for doing so. Women were "scarce" in the territory (six men to each woman) and there was hope that a bill for women's voting rights would draw more women to the area. There was also the hope that once women were enfranchised, they would vote for the party that had given them the vote to begin with. (Imagine the legislators' chagrin when a majority of the 1,000 women who participated in that September 1870 election voted Republican.) The Democrats in the legislature also wanted to put the Republican governor in a tight spot—the thinking was the governor would probably veto the bill, showing that, even though the Republicans advocated for voting rights for ex-slaves, they would not extend the same rights to women. There were also stories that the whole thing was a joke, and no one expected that the idea would really take hold and become law.

Arguments abounded against giving women the vote. I included some of those arguments—and the refutations—in this story. You can read some of the common 19th century arguments against women's suffrage in the online Slate article, "Common 19th Century Arguments Against Women's Suffrage, Neatly Refuted," by Rebecca Onion.

So, did men stop their wives from voting, or tell them how to vote? You may not read about it in the newspapers of the day, but I have no doubt that such voter suppression existed. In fact, my paternal grandfather bragged once that "She [my grandmother] votes the way I tell her to." Even though I was very young when he said this—probably nine or ten years old—his comment stuck with me, and decades later, became the creative engine that drove this story. Voter suppression? Indeed. And at the most personal, intimate level.

About Ann Parker

Ann Parker earned degrees in Physics and English Literature at the University of California, Berkeley, before taking up a career as a science writer. These days, she slings science and technical verbiage for a living during the day and writes fiction at night.

Ann's ancestors include a great-grandfather who was a blacksmith in Leadville, a grandmother who worked at the bindery of Leadville's *Herald Democrat* newspaper, a grandfather who was a Colorado School of Mines professor, and another grandfather who worked as a gandy dancer on the Colorado railroads. She is a member of the National Association of Science Writers, the Mystery Writers of America, Sisters in Crime, International Thriller Writers, Historical Novel Society, Women Writing the West, and Western Writers of America. Ann and her family reside in the San Francisco Bay Area, whence they have weathered numerous boom-and-bust cycles.

Her Silver Rush historical mystery series, published by Poisoned Pen Press, is set in the silver boomtown of Leadville, Colorado, in the early 1880s. The series was picked as a "Booksellers Favorite" by the Mountains and Plains Independent Booksellers Association.

For more about Ann Parker, see http:// www.annparker.net.

ABSENTEE

ALISON CATHARINE

MADDIE SAUNTERED UP THE EMPTY steep driveway. The pumpkin-colored truck her father washed each weekend, drought be damned, with the radio on turn-it-down volume, and a cup of tea teetering on its curved roof was recuperating down at the shop. Her father was inside arguing with the TV, she could hear, and singing along with the ads. "We're stranded," her mother had claimed, a mild panic spiraling through the phone. Or free, Maddie thought.

Also absent were the full-size fake tombstones and rental speakers which just last week had blasted thunder at costumed children begging for candy. Now, a well-dressed scarecrow with newsboy cap and a Union Jack scarf chased cardboard turkeys with a butterfly net. Straw was strewn around the neatly clipped lawn outside her parents' bungalow on Coral Lane. Still something else was going on.

"Has he lost his mind?" their neighbor shouted from the street. To her surprised face, he pointed across the lawn, next to a small white cross beneath the willow tree. The cross was there every year, for Tommy. But today, between the scarecrow's feet and the tree was a political candidate's sign. A large red sign for that power-hungry, hawkish candidate that most in the state thought was not only clinically crazy but destructive.

"He's not voting for that guy, is he? Your Dad?"

Maddie shrugged. With her hand inside her pocket, she flipped off both the neighbor and the sign. Usually the neighbors just said hello, asked her what play was being put on next. Then would come that awkward request for free tickets, which they could boast about to their friends.

"Have a nice day," she hollered after the man. Another neighbor took her picture.

The first neighbor trundled off with his small dog shuffling like a floor mop down the spotless asphalt. The other ducked back inside a home. Wild deer nonplussed by people ate at another neighbor's lawn, popping up their chewing faces to watch the kerfuffle.

She wished Dan was here, quipping about this being the close of act one, tension building, the villain just off-stage. Maddie knocked on the front door. Getting no answer, she opened the door with her key and called out.

"In here, Mad. We're in here."

"You two have been busy. You ready for lift-off?"

"I saw her plucking cowslips and marked her where she stood/," her father sang. *"She never knew I watched her while hiding in the wood"*

"Halloween's over, Dad, judging by your lawn. And that

hasn't scared me since I was eight." She left the front door open, expecting to be in and out.

Dropping her purse against the wall, she stopped in the hallway to hide a shiver; she hated that poem. She touched the photo of her brother on the side table. The triangular frame with his folded American flag leaned behind it. It'd been ten years, but there was Tommy, forever young and heroic. Bastard, she thought.

The hallway gave way to a den festooned with projects for friends and neighbors. Always a few, today Maddie counted over twenty. This can't go on much longer, she thought, at their age. Amongst it all sat her parents, like children after opening gifts on Christmas Day: one thankful, the other, fuming with a nugget of coal. She approached the happy parent first.

"You two dancing in the moonlight again?" Maddie teased. Her mother sat with a bandaged ankle elevated on the sofa, still in a nightgown on this Tuesday afternoon.

"In the kitchen usually, dear. But no, just the bad kind of trip. The bruise has already turned green. I'm on the mend."

"Years in this country, Mom. You still talk funny," Maddie crossed in front of them to open the deck door, to ease the room's stuffiness. Cool damp air blew in around her.

"You're blocking the TV. Move," her father shouted. Perched on the edge of a chair, he was trying to balance a neighbor's cat tree. A guitar and strings laid next to him. Another project, Maddie assumed, as none of them played. Maddie sat next to her mother, peering at her ankle.

"You're supposed to wear those black boots all the time, Mom, even inside the house. They keep your ankles secure. You weren't wearing them, were you?"

"I forbid that to happen," her father shouted.

"What? You can't forbid it, Dad. You don't have any say in it, the doctors' do," Maddie clenched her fist playfully at him.

"Not that, this," he hinted at a smile then pointed to the TV. "They say your person is up in the polls. That they might win. Not in my state."

"Is it really such a bad thing your guy might lose?" Maddie asked.

Her mother directed them all to her healthy foot. "I'm wearing one of them," she lifted up her nightie to reveal a thick ankle boot.

"Very risqué there, Mom. Showing all kinds of shin."

Her mother pretended to blush and dropped a newspaper onto the pile near her foot. Maddie estimated a week's worth were spread around the den, with takeout food containers on top of them. Exhaling through her nose, Maddie tried to push away the competing odors.

"This and the truck's demise have really interrupted our humdrum life, right Eliot?"

"You're using that word again, Mom." She rose to pick up the papers.

"We use it because you dislike it, silly! So strange, to hate a word," her father said. The cat tree's base was solid. Still the upper section tilted too far to support a finicky Fluffy or Mittens. He examined that, trying to add a counterbalance.

"Humdrum just sounds so schoolroom spelling test," Maddie said looking outside.

On the road just beyond the yard, children shouted as they rode bicycles up makeshift ramps to leap through the air. Tommy had done that, she remembered, once even riding his bicycle up a ramp in the backyard and over the small stream onto the road. The bike's silhouette against the sky had looked like some prehistoric bird escaping its demise.

"You never realize how much you need a car until it's gone," her mother sighed.

"Is that what drove this room falling apart?" She picked up the last of the papers and a few of the food containers and headed for the kitchen. When she looked back, her mother was shaking her head. Maddie mouthed "what?" but was ignored.

"What is wrong with everyone?" Her father yelled. The news showed his candidate calling people names and being called names by the press.

"We don't have a problem, Dad. It's him. And you can't forbid it. Freedom of the press."

"They're not treating him fairly."

"You can't always vote with the party line, Dad. You have to look at the gray area."

"Don't give him grief, Mad. Not today...with the truck," her mother stated.

Maddie put everything in the garage's bins. She knew why they held onto Tommy's truck but she had different memories. In high school it was called the "virgin slayer." Every weekend the two of them – Tommy and her father – would be out there washing it. Tommy always so proud of how little he paid: it had belonged to a roofing company who agreed to the price because Tommy wasn't going to paint over their phone number on the side. With every mile, they got free advertising. With every mile, Tommy's list of trysts grew. On her phone, her parents left messages for Tommy, because he claimed to be with her. Even now, with her father driving it around, the company got calls. None of them threats from cuckolded men, however.

"I'm not going with you today, it's just errands," he said.

"I'm not leaving your mother with those people out there. Rabid dogs."

"I only met one neighbor and he was annoyed. But your lawn sign?"

"I have a right to my opin—"

"I'll show you where the list is, Mad." Her mother hobbled towards the kitchen, reaching for the list on the refrigerator.

"Mom, you shouldn't be walking on that."

"I'm only walking a little ways. I need you to drop your father's shirts off at the cleaners, then go to Frankie's Flicks and return these DVDs."

"You can rent these online cheaper than what she charges. I've shown you." Maddie picked up the bag full of recycling from the kitchen floor and walked it to the garage.

"We like going to Frankie's. She knows so much, and I don't want to 'look it up.'"

"She told us about that film you liked, that British radio one about the war. We watched it the last time you were here," her father hollered.

"You guys can watch modern films, you know. The war is over!"

"There's so much swearing, and violence. And robots. And super powers. And everyone keeps yelling at each other," he shouted from the living room. Maddie and her mother avoided eye contact so they didn't laugh.

"And the people don't talk anymore," her father added.

Maddie had to nod her head in agreement. Earlier she'd left Dan in the midst of discussing where to spend their anniversary. He was now up in wine country building a stage set, a 'storefront church' he said, and being paid in cases of wine. He had left a drunken message singing Cher in a falsetto, asking Maddie if she 'believed in love.' When she texted back that she'd believe in anything after a couple of glasses, he'd sent her a GIF of Pepe le Pew's eyes bursting into hearts at the sight of some lovely faux skunk. Then he asked if she could 'turn back time' and sent a photo from their honeymoon of her in a bikini. Maddie had turned off the phone.

"Also mail our absentee ballots. We forgot to," her mother said.

"*Remember, remember the fifth of November/. . .*" her father sang. "*A penn'orth of cheese to choke him/A pint of beer to wash it down/And a jolly good fire to burn him down . . .*"

"The incumbent isn't that bad, Dad." She clapped the dust off her hands. The sound echoed in the cool garage, full of finished projects. "I'll mail yours, Mom. I'm not mailing his."

"Yes you will!" His voice boomed wide in the dark space. Maddie entered the kitchen and shut the garage door behind her. The ballots sat with the bills, ready for postal flight. Her mother leaned on the counter and mouthed for her to just mail them. Maddie filled the empty dishwasher, anything but talk. Back in the den, she picked up the remaining food containers.

"I'll stay here with Mom and you can walk the eight blocks to the mailbox, or into town. That way you know she's safe. They pick up at 3:00 PM, don't they? That gives you an hour. In town, it's a 5:00pm pick up. You've plenty of time."

Her father waved her away. "Not going anywhere without the truck."

"You can take my car, Dad."

He peered around her at the TV and joined in singing the praises of Mr. Clean. Maddie walked away and let the kitchen tap run until the water rose in temperature. As it filled the tub, she asked her mother: "How long have you two been doing this? With the food and the papers?"

Her mother shook her head. "Four days now. The truck broke down on the road. Sargent Collins found your father crying by it and brought him home."

"Collins? He didn't come into the house, did he?"

"You've never liked that man. Just because he had a wild youth. He's much changed. He even called to see how your father was doing. Your father just kept asking about the truck."

"Why did Collins call?"

"He was being nice, Mad. Your father didn't even notice my ankle until he was on the phone with Sargent Collins. He's better with the news distracting him."

"I think the TV should be turned off, Mom. It's making him worse."

"Well the truck will be ready tomorrow," she turned to hobble back toward the den. "You remember when Tommy let you drive it out to Stinson Beach? Around those curves? Tommy said you looked like Grace Kelly with your scarf on, driving around the roads of Monaco. He raved that people took pictures of you, like you were already famous."

Her mother picked at some chipped paint on the kitchen's door. "You always look so happy in the papers or on TV. Why doesn't that person ever come to visit?"

Maddie dropped her hands into the sink's hot water, splashing it up on herself.

"Tommy was doing better, opening up in that group, they said." Limping closer, her mother whispered. "You know your father still thinks you were driving that night."

She turned off the tap and stared at her mother, hot water dripping onto her sneakered feet. "I'm not talking about this again. And you just answered your earlier question."

Her mother returned to the den. Maddie threw the sponge against the window. It bounced back into the hot water unaffected. Drying her hands, she put the bills, the list, and her mother's absentee ballot in her purse. She placed her father's on the hallway table. A cool cross breeze came from the front door; she imagined it going through her. The tv was shut off. The sudden silence hurt Maddie's ears.

"Tell me this, Dad. Did you really vote for him? Or someone else? I don't care who – just not him."

"He was part of the cabinet that sent your brother over there. And brought him back. If I don't vote for him, your brother...would never forgive me."

"Dad, even the people who sent Tommy over there don't like this guy. Tommy would've hated this guy. He—"

"You don't know that." He marched past her to the table, grabbed the ballot and shoved it at her. "Mail it!"

As he did the photo frame fell onto the floor. Glass shattered and slid across the wood, resting by their feet. She stared at it unsurprised, while her father dropped to his knees, apologizing. Maddie bent to remove the frame from his hand. When he refused to let go, she picked up his ballot, and leaned it against the wall. "I'll get the dustpan. Don't move. Glass."

"I'm not doing wrong by him, Lizzie. I'm not." He clutched the frame to his chest. As she walked away, her mother approached.

"Eliot. Please, come over here and sit down. I'm sure Maddie will post them," her mother said, steadying herself with a hand on the wall.

"He gave up everything, Mad. What have you done?

Pretend to be other people?"

Maddie stopped still. She threw the dustpan and brush on the ground at his knees. "Nothing? You want to know what happened that night? He called me yet again to cover for him. And this time he'd committed a crime. An actual crime."

"Mad, this is no time for your stories," her mother dismissed. "Help your father up."

Maddie continued. "He and his buddy robbed someone at gunpoint! That's not a story."

"How dare you say that about your brother," her father slowly stood up. Her mother teetered beside him, staring past Maddie.

"He wasn't jogging each morning, Mom. He couldn't sleep inside. He was waking up after you two had gone to bed and sleeping in his truck. Those were night sweats each morning, not his breaking the six-minute mile."

Her mother's face registered a knowing, like when deciphering a crossword puzzle. Her father took a step backwards, color rising up his neck, then started forward. As he did, he bumped both the table and her mother, putting her off balance. He reached out to steady her, to protect. Instead, down she went, Maddie saw, a red mark on her face, her father looming above. But what the neighbors heard was a woman shriek, a man yell, and a call to arms went out.

Later Maddie would recall how the rest of the day had occurred in slow motion; an elongated denouement begun when her mother turned off the TV. Neighbors outside would later tell the police they saw it all – standing on their tiptoes, Maddie reasoned, peering with their X-ray vision into the unlit hallway—and that her father should be arrested.

But first that neighbor from earlier was at the door. "What's happened? What did he do?"

"Nothing. He fell and then she fell," Maddie briskly closed the door in the man's face.

"I'm so sorry, Lizzie," her father said.

They wobbled to their feet. Together they walked back towards the den, peppering the floor with minute blood drops, then with light red stripes.

"Mom, stop walking. Look at your foot. Sit down."

Noticing the blood, her father hollered. "See what you've done, Mad!"

She looked at the ceiling as her father escorted her mother away from her. As Maddie swept up the shards, she watched him pick each piece of glass out of her bare foot. With caution and care, he used a damp towel to wash away blood. Her mother kept saying she was alright, not to make a fuss. However, once he sat down and reached for her hand, she clasped it tightly.

Her parents stayed silent as Maddie wiped the hallway floor. The sounds of children playing daredevil games wafted in through the open back door.

"He didn't do what you said, did he?" her mother asked.

"Don't...answer that," her father said, the frame still in hand.

"I have proof," she said quietly. Then red lights twirled across the den's wall; a knock on the front door; an ambulance outside. That neighbor, that pivotal brief on-stage character, had called the police. Standing, her palms and back sweaty, Maddie opened the front door.

During the whirl of questions that followed, men and women in uniforms tramped through the small home, army ants knocking things over and joining together to put them back in place: other frames, that flag in its triangle. At each mishap, Maddie watched her parents deflate like a birthday balloon. To Maddie, the police asked about elder care and if she felt threatened or burdened. Her raucous laugh, when she heard it, made her think of a Disney villain.

As the police wrapped up, Maddie stood outside in the backyard. A perfect square, it had been her first stage. The staircase into it where the audience, her family, or Dan had sat. The flowerbeds on either side of the staircase were the faceless crowds in the cheap seats. The wind through the trees, the roar of that crowd. She wondered if it was all about to end. And Dan, what about Dan, she thought, her hand across her mouth. She thought of leaving it all as is, keeping it once again in the family; the noise of that crowd began to scream within her.

At the stairs' underbelly, beneath its highest step, she squatted and dug in the dirt. Dandelions had grown there. Covered in faded stickers of music bands, Tommy's gray metal box emerged from the earth; it used to hold mementos of girlfriends, sometimes weed. Opening it, she saw everything from that night and her stomach clenched with remembered fear. Still in there, as always, were three plastic daisies from the basket of her first bike; Tommy always said they brought him luck. He didn't take them with him on his last tour. She closed the lid, holding the box with two hands as she had that night, and climbed the stairs towards the police.

Tommy had called her after midnight back then. Got her up and out to the empty land one block from her in-laws' house, where she and Dan were visiting. Early summer, she had thrown on the prior day's sundress to dash out. He'd run himself off the road, "racing memories" he'd said when she arrived. They argued under the streetlamp about his re-enlisting; she said he was too old, he said he missed it, the front, life here was humdrum.

"Humdrum? For real?" Maddie recalled. "What's that? Where did that come from?"

He wouldn't look at where she pointed: the gun and cash in the grey box, open in the front seat. "This guy from the vet's group. He wanted help. This one-time thing. That's my cut."

"What! Tommy, those never work out. In the movies." Maddie stepped away from the truck. "Your stupid women, all those phone calls from Mom and Dad. Fine. Not this."

"Look you're so good with stories. I know it was stupid. Tell me what to say," he pleaded. "It hasn't even been fired. We took the money from Eddie Collins. He was so drunk and stoned he didn't even see. We wore masks. Come on, they'll be here soon."

"Who will be here?"

He crossed his arms, hands shoved under the armpits. "The cops. New station is up the road, remember? Always drive this way end of a shift."

"Why did you park here then? I would've met you, wherever you were."

Tommy's glassy eyes started to water, and his face lost its composure. "Stop yelling at me. I always talk to them at night. Right here. I'd miss them if they didn't stop by. Maybe I should start walking that plank now." He held his arms out at his sides and walked a line.

"You are such a sad sack when you're drunk, Tommy."

After a few steps, he dropped his arms. "I can't go to prison. Those walls, that small space. And they'll know, you know, if they find me with this stuff. Look, Mr. Collins' has those fancy money wrappers with the store's name on it and everything," he pointed at the box.

"You should've thought of this first! I can't believe you...wait. God, you didn't commit it in this truck? The one everyone knows?"

"Come on, just this last time, for me," he walked around the front of the truck and looked her in the eyes with a tenderness Maddie knew was reserved for his women. "Please."

If only, she had thought afterwards. But she hadn't a lock with her. She could've put it on the box and left it with him. He would've been put away. Maybe the Collins family might've been lenient if the money was returned. Maybe Eddie Collins back then, Sargent Collins now, might not have joined the police. But she dared not leave the gun. Not with him in this state.

She took it all back then and walked away. She dropped the bottle in the field and emptied the weed out of the bag as she walked. Not long afterwards, she crouched down amongst the tree roots, as one policeman made Tommy walk the drunken line. The other—fancying himself Dirty Harry—kept pointing his gun at different trees. When he pointed at where she hid, she stopped breathing. As they drove past, Tommy headed to the drunk tank, she froze, eyes level with the high beams. Once alone, she kicked a tree until her toes hurt. A few leaves fell around her; she slapped them away. The next day, she hid the box back where Tommy had kept it when younger. They never spoke again. Maddie left a few days later for filming in Los Angeles. She ignored his apologetic messages; then he re-enlisted; then he was dead.

Now Maddie re-entered the house. She set the box, contents intact, on the floor next to her purse. Both parents were being taken out to the ambulance, her mother in a gurney. Just to check them out, the EMTs said. Exiting, her mother grabbed her wrist.

"Where did you get that? It was a story, wasn't it? What you said."

Maddie shook her head. "What do you think happened back then?"

"That you had been out drinking and called him for a ride. But you, being you, insisted you were fine, insisted on driving. Then he pretended to be drunk, to let you get away."

"Mom, if I had been caught drunk driving, I would've gone to rehab, done community service, come out a winner. Like all those actresses you dislike."

Her mother's eyes registered surprise. Her voice dropped in timbre. "I wouldn't have hated you. If that had happened."

Looking around the bungalow, Maddie imagined the glass in every frame, in every bottle and in the drinking glasses themselves shattering. A glass house, she thought, collapsed. "You thought that of me for ten years?" Maddie removed her wrist. "That I let Tommy take the fall?"

"You two always had your secrets. We didn't know. Don't say anything, please."

The EMTs took her mother out through the front door. Maddie gathered her belongings, including the box. Climbing into the ambulance behind the gurney, her father still held the frame tight to his chest. The congregating neighbors were quiet. Maddie wondered if it was from weariness, or compassion, or even sadly, happiness at the scene they were witnessing.

As the ambulance doors closed, another police car pulled up. Out of it emerged Sargent Collins. Unsmiling he walked past the ambulance and spoke a few minor words to an EMT. He grew taller upon his approach to Maddie, until he towered over her. "Hello, Mad. Nice to see you. We're going to take them in—"

"Take them in? They didn't do anything!"

He put his hands out, palms facing her. She saw the scar sustained when as a teenager, he tried to join Tommy in jumping their bikes over the stream and instead fell in. Collins had landed on a market shopping cart, requiring numerous stitches and forever etching a grid pattern scar on one hand. He was called Bagger and Checker for years which did everything to inspire his career choices. "Wrong words. To the hospital. Gardening?"

He pointed to her dirt-covered hands. She lay the box and ballots on the driveway and wiped her hands on the lawn. "Nope."

"Those the culprits?" Collins pointed at the absentee ballots.

She looked at the lawn sign, the cardboard turkeys, anywhere but at Collins. Picking up the box and ballots, she stage-whispered. "Nope."

He laughed. A warm laugh, she thought, for a local policeman, like from that old TV show the kid Ron Howard was in, hokey and kind. "Tommy always said you were a terrible liar. Single word answers, never looking people in the face. Let me give you a ride to the hospital."

"That lawn sign better be there when we get back." Maddie yelled at the neighbors after the ambulance left. She felt her face turn as red as a turkey's snood. She reached for the police car's back door, where the perps sat. Collins opened the front door instead.

"This isn't Hollywood, Mad. I'm not your chauffeur."

"Course not. My mistake. I have to mail these."

He nodded and kept chatting as she climbed in. "Telling stories though, telling those tall tales. Tommy used to say you could 'grow trees in the air'. Got a good one for the ride?"

"Yes. Yes I do."

About the Songs

Dad sings lyrics from two real songs in this story:

I saw her plucking cowslips and marked her where she stood
She never knew I watched her while hiding in the wood
— from "The Witch", Percy H. Ilott

Remember, remember the fifth of November
A penn'orth of cheese to choke him
A pint of beer to wash it down
And a jolly good fire to burn him down
— from "The Fifth of November", English folk verse

About Alison Catharine

Alison Catharine has an MFA from University of San Francisco, and has written several novels and short stories in multiple genres, including crime and literary fiction. She has a gift for exploring how world events affect family relationships. Alison's unsentimental kindness and incisive observation inform all her work.

CHICAGO STYLE

DAVID HAGERTY

EVERYONE IN CHICAGO KNEW ABOUT the Machine. For two decades, no one got a business license or a civil service job without showing obeisance to its mayor, Richard J. Daley, and offering patronage to his party. Statewide he made out the Democratic ticket then got out the voters to support it. Legend held that he even swung the 1960 election to J.F.K.

But during the 1978 gubernatorial primary, an insurgent rose to challenge him. Duncan Cochrane, who'd made his fortune in salted pork but possessed no political experience, declared his candidacy for Illinois' state house without receiving the blessing of the Second City's ruler. Problem was, Chicago housed almost half the state's Democrats, so anyone vying for office needed its backing. How could a businessman, a neophyte, for God's sake, beat the town's monarch?

"No dirty tactics," Duncan told his campaign manager, Kai Soto.

Like Duncan, Kai was an outsider, a recent transplant from California. His Japanese roots and samurai's ponytail alienated him from the party's Irish establishment, who ridiculed his bell bottoms and velour shirts, branding him a Left Coast disco diva.

"The locals will tell you, politics ain't bean-bag," Kai replied. "Just because you play fair doesn't mean the Machine will. We've got to fight with our elbows and knees."

It remained an unsettled debate among the campaign staff whether the City that Works (in the mayor's words) could be reformed, or, in the words of The Who, "History ain't changed."

Early on, Duncan had sought the mayor's support, visiting "The Hall" where he kept a spartan office. His broad mahogany desk bore only a phone and a bust of Honest Abe Lincoln. Two flags flanked him, America's and Chicago's, holding equal rank.

To look at him, you'd never know the power Daley held. He embodied his working class upbringing, with diction from the stockyards and a bungalow near his parents' in Bridgeport. Squat and jowly, he hardly intimidated, sitting erect and stiff in his green leather chair, hands folded on his desktop like a dutiful pupil. Of course, the same could be said of many generations of the Chicago Outfit, the mob that had organized everything from Prohibition to prostitution, often with the tacit consent of City Hall.

"You live in the suburbs," the mayor said.

"Now, yes, but I grew up in River Park."

"You've got a business in Back of the Yards."

"Packaged meats. Hot dogs, sausages, bratwurst. Started it twenty years ago. Built it from two employees into two hundred."

The mayor frowned and shook his head with approval. "Hog butcher for the world." He recited more line items—business license, rezoning, donations to the party—without notes or prompts, using statements, not questions, as though he'd memorized Duncan's résumé.

"We catered many meetings for your precinct captains," Duncan said.

Again, Daley frowned his endorsement. "Now you want to get into politics."

"Public service. I'm blessed with good business sense. I want to share that with the state."

"And you want my support."

Duncan nodded, feigning humility.

"Even though I never got yours."

Duncan leaned forward until the big man's broad desk stopped him. "I always donated to the party. I attended your fundraisers, met with your block captains."

Daley rubbed his hands together as though trying to cleanse them of something tacky and foul. "You did what you had to do. No more, no less."

"I had a business to run, a family to look after. At the time, I didn't see myself in politics."

The mayor's hands turned as red as if he'd been washing them under scalding water. "You really think you can beat Big Bill Stratton? The governor has a massive war chest and a barnyard of loyal voters downstate."

"Which is why I need your help."

Daley nodded, frowning. "If I back you, how do I know you'll be loyal?"

"I've been a Democrat all my life, always voted for the party, gave to JFK's campaign and LBJ's, even to Carter's."

"None of which helps the city of Chicago. I've got people who've worked in our organization for forty years, ever since they could pull a voting lever, who never asked such a favor."

"Not a favor. An endorsement. Nothing more than your name backing me."

Daley frowned, promised to give it "his consideration." Instead, he slated his own candidate to the liberal ticket and threw the Machine's support behind him.

That winter a grey overcast tinged the city and the campaign. Duncan studied newspaper photos and TV footage of his opponent for evidence of conspiracy. He found plenty. As a city alderman, Mitch Kupcinek practiced at dissembling. He denied not just the Machine's influence but its existence. "There is no Machine. There are only people loyal to the party," he said. Yet that word "loyalty" echoed the mayor's own term, one that would resonate in the ears of every civil servant and partisan.

Kupcinek embodied the ward politics that organized the city. The thirty-second bore Polish roots and allegiances, so he drank lager at Jakub's pub, bought sausages at Kovak's deli, prayed at St. Hedwig's. He got a loading zone for the local butcher and a liquor license for the neighborhood market. He fixed their parking tickets and their building citations, and in exchange, they voted however he wanted.

Now the Machine was backing his reach toward the governor's office. Overnight, thousands of his signs appeared around town, so numerous it would take half of the civil service to install them all, bearing the slogan "vote the party's choice" in the pale blue, white and red of the city flag. Simultaneously, Duncan's own billboards disappeared. One news stationed filmed a city crew tearing them down. When asked, the sanitation director said that they violated local ordinances, though he wouldn't say how.

Daley wanted one of his own running the state capital. If Kupcinek won, Chicago controlled all of Illinois. Downstate voters recognized the power grab and opposed him, supporting Duncan by default. Yet they numbered barely half the state's Democrats. Even if every farmer from Peoria joined every renegade from the city, the Machine could manufacture enough fraudulent ballots to nullify their votes.

Kai and Duncan started their uprising at the state board of elections, which occupied an entire floor of a skyscraper downtown, with views of the Sears Tower and the Chicago River. Despite its luxury, the board had only recently joined the roll call of public agencies, formed by Gov. Stratton less than a decade earlier as a statewide check against voter fraud. Pundits assumed he was targeting the Second City and its leader, but they doubted its efficacy: Mark Rica of the *Daily News* labeled them "the incapable crusaders."

The board's director, Benjamin Sauterne, kept an ornate conference room accessorized with a rosewood table and matching chairs. He wore equally elaborate attire: a custom three-piece suit that flattered his thin frame, and designer cologne that masked his thin essence. The comforts he enjoyed worried Duncan. He needed someone young, cynical, aggressive, to check all the shenanigans of the Machine.

"We're quite familiar with Chicago's ways," said the director.

Compared to many locals, who tortured their vowels into

oblongs, his speech offered exaggerated diction, as though he'd spent his adolescence in an English boarding school. His attitude projected similar polish, his legs crossed at the knee, hands folded in his lap. All he lacked was a brandy snifter.

"How can you supervise an election from here?" Duncan said, gesturing to the climate controlled suites around them. "You need to watch the barrooms and union halls, keep out the repeaters and floaters who stuff the ballot boxes at a dozen different polling stations."

"Everyone has a right to vote," said the director. "Our job is to ensure that their votes are tallied accurately, is it not?"

"Last election, the polls tallied ten thousand dead people. How will you count *them* accurately?"

The other man leaned back as though settling in for a tedious lesson with a daft pupil. "Have faith," he said. He fingered a silver crucifix that hung from his neck with the savior looking beatified.

"Faith in what?" Duncan said. As a Presbyterian, he never put much stock in the accouterments of righteousness, instead counting on the Protestant work ethic.

"Dare I say that the era of bribery and fraud has passed," Sauterne said. "Need I remind you of the Shakman decrees, which effectively ended political patronage in city government. It freed people to vote their consciences, free of influence from their bosses or shop stewards."

"Someone needs to explain that to the Machine."

In the car ride back from his office, Duncan debriefed with his chief aide.

"Is that man as gullible as he sounds?"

Kai steered calmly through heavy traffic along Wacker Drive, which paralleled the river through a channel of skyscrapers. "It's his role to project confidence. To acknowledge all the chicanery he sees but can't stop would force him out of character."

"So you think he's acting?"

"The only way to play that role is as a straight man to a farce."

As a theater major, Kai viewed politics in dramatic terms, often following a tragic model.

"A polite lie in place of a rude truth," Duncan said.

"It's the only justification for the board's existence."

The cars in front of them settled to an idle, pooling their exhaust with the grey overcast, while people honked their impatience. By the sidewalk stood a traffic cop arrayed in loyalist blues. He ignored the mess in front of him until Kai rolled down his window to inquire about the delay.

"Dey're staging for da parade," he said in typical Chicago brogue.

"Parade?" Duncan said. He scanned ahead to see floats and marching bands slowly funneling into State Street, then noted the green tinge of the river. Each St. Patrick's Day the mayor led the procession, accompanied by other politicians and officials whom he favored. No doubt, Kupcinek would walk by his side carrying the banner of the party.

"Why didn't we get an invitation?" Duncan said.

Kai shook his head. "Wrong lineage."

Their next stop lay on the near North Side, a watering hole and tavern called the Mirage. Its exterior looked anything but tempting: a glass storefront with burglar bars and neon beer signs. Inside it proved no more fantastic, with an aroma of smoke and mildew, and the steady hiss of ancient radiators. Its name referred instead to its operation as a front for the Better Government Association, a cabal of journalists and do-gooders bent on reforming city government. They'd purchased the beer hall for a sting to ferret out crooked city bureaucrats, but now that the story had broken, the place sat empty and unused.

Behind the bar stood Pamela Zekman, a reporter for the *Sun-Times* who'd paid for the honey pot with her own funds. Thus, she could reserve it for confidential interviews like that with Duncan and Kai, her only two customers. She could have been anyone's neighbor, with a small frame and big hair, except for her defiant stare.

"I get something for you?" she said.

"An honest election," Duncan said as he sat on a wobbly bar stool.

"There's a high price for that." She smiled her dead smile and set out three glasses of seltzer water with lime.

"That's my concern," Duncan said. He chugged his drink, stifled a belch, and waited for the effervescence to subside. "Anything you can do to keep it clean?"

She pointed at the wall separating front from back. "See that?"

Duncan studied the wood paneling but saw only cheap décor.

"Behind there's the hidden camera we used to out corruption in City Hall. We recorded dozens of inspectors soliciting bribes for all this." She gestured to the exposed wires and damaged ceiling behind her, fishing lures to graft.

"You think guerrilla tactics can work in a polling place?"

"It caught a third of the building department."

"Daley's got thirty-five thousand city workers who

depend on his largesse. Not to mention most of the businessmen in town. How can you catch them all?"

"We use other ways, too."

"Such as?"

She refilled his glass before explaining. "We know their tactics, just not where and when they'll deploy them. After the fact, news leaks out. Precinct captains and party workers brag to their friends, who tell two friends, and so on, until the whole town knows. We just have to wait for the ripples to reach land."

"By which time we will have lost."

"Not necessarily," Kai said. "We could use the news to force a recount."

"Overseen by the same people who perpetrated the fraud."

"The Machine's bolts are weakened, ready to give with enough pressure," said the barkeep. "You could be the wrench that frees the last screw."

Or I could get screwed, Duncan thought.

With so little assurance of a fair election, Duncan and Kai agreed they needed to fight with equal craft. If the Machine planned to stuff the ballot boxes, they needed a filling of their own.

In desperation, they travelled to Operation PUSH to see its charismatic leader, Jesse Jackson. His office overlooked the streets of Kenwood, a working class neighborhood on the city's hardscrabble South Side. Through the windows drifted the aroma of sweet potato pie, along with a funky horn and conga tune, urging listeners to "Move on Up." In keeping with his roots, the minister wore an inexpensive suit, plus his characteristic afro and mustache.

Before either of his guests could state their agenda, he

sermonized for twenty minutes about disenfranchisement and plebiscites. Throughout his voice rose with moral outrage, and he punctuated his rhetoric with rhyming couplets too perfect to be improvised. He concluded by threatening to PUSH his supporters to the Republicans in the general election if the plantation wards on the South Side, where white overseers ruled majority black electorates, were not fairly counted.

Once the reverend had ended his diatribe, Duncan dared to speak. "We want what you want: a true accounting. If you can rally your people to support me, I can—"

"Mr. Cochrane, do you know how many politicians have come to my house, begging my support, never to return again?"

"I'm not a politician. I'm a businessman, one who understands the importance of relationships—"

"If you're campaigning for office, you are prima facie a politician."

Duncan leaned forward to lower his voice. "As are you. You may deliver your speeches from the altar, but they are as surely political as anything I say."

At that, the activist leaned back and steepled his fingers as he studied his foil. "How do we know you're not some boll weevil Democrat who speaks the language of liberation while advocating the policies of segregation?"

"Because I'm opposing the Machine that built this city into what it is today."

The reverend nodded, pondered, and replied, "Do you know why I begin and end my speeches with the phrase 'I am somebody?' Because so few of our brothers and sisters believe that they matter, that their votes matter."

Duncan stood to punctuate his final words. "If you can

convince them that they do, I can make it so."

Still, turnout at Duncan's campaign events proved modest: some friends and business associates, people whose votes he expected. With the electorate playing coy, the candidate needed a direct approach.

So on weekends he walked door to door, stumping in the wealthy parts of town—Lincoln Park and the Gold Coast —where people did not depend on the Machine for their sustenance. Even with all the graft and corruption, few civil servants could afford high rises or Victorians near the lakefront.

Most of these interactions proved discouraging. People responded: "I never vote" "why bother" and worst "who?" One older gentleman, with glasses that pinched his face into a scowl, asked skeptically, "You're not one of Daley's boys?" By himself, Duncan could never convert enough believers.

So his family joined. To appeal to the housewives, his wife Josie wore a wrap from I. Magnin, a bouffant worthy of Margaret Thatcher, and Chanel No. 5. His children travelled together, promoting their father's family values. Aden was in the throes of his awkward adolescence, with floppy hair and a sullen temperament, but Lindsay had received the polish of a Vassar education. With her blond hair and cover girl smile, people compared her to Lindsay Wagner, the Bionic Woman. She'd need similar powers to make headway.

When they expanded their canvas to the bungalow belt, which housed Daley's army of civil servants, many voters refused to open their doors or to accept their literature, as though they feared any association with a rebellion. One woman said simply, "I can't." They heeded the unspoken message of the Machine: "Keep your mouth shut."

After one canvas, in which they had walked the entire twenty stories of a high rise downtown without securing a single vote, Duncan prepared his family for the inevitable. They reconnoitered outside, where cars along Lake Shore Drive sprayed slush and noise.

"Not that I don't appreciate you help," Duncan said, "but you don't need to spend all your weekends stumping for me."

"What's more important than ensuring your victory?" said Josie.

"I wish I felt so confident."

"You should, daddy," said Lindsay. "People will support you once they know you."

Aden snorted his disagreement.

"What?" said his sister.

"You're such a Goody Two-shoes."

"Because I believe in him?"

"Because you don't get that the game is fixed."

"No negativity," said their mother. "If we persist, we will win."

That ethic worked well in business, where wooing customers trumped threatening them, but few salesmen could intimidate like the Cook County Democrats did.

On election night, Duncan retreated to a suite at the Drake, a luxurious hotel on the Magnificent Mile that had hosted princes and presidents. Knowing not what to expect, he watched the three local news broadcasts simultaneously. The latest polls called the race a dead heat, but they did not account for malfeasance. Evidence suggested that the Chicago style prevailed. Early footage showed four-legged voters— those accompanied by a loyalist to ensure they pulled the correct levers—and hobo floto voto—those same partisans leading vagrants by one shaky hand to the polling stations. Rumors spread that the Machine had churned out walking around money to all its patronage workers.

In the ballroom downstairs waited hundreds of Duncan's supporters, who feasted on meaty canapés and sparkling cider, anticipating the appearance of their savior, but the candidate would not face them until he knew which speech to read: of celebration or concession. Once polling stations closed and early returns leaked out, his anxiety built. The news anchors still declared the race as too close to call.

He drank a scotch, then another, and requested a third when Josie stopped him. "This should be your most sober moment," she said.

The candidate doubted it, but complied.

For the next several hours, he skipped between channels, seeking some encouragement, hearing instead more evidence of fraud. Election workers sorted ballots with careless disregard. Black voters complained of being turned away from the polls. Mitch Kupcinek appeared, preaching patience with a mischievous grin. The head of the local elections board proclaimed his dedication to counting every last ballot, then refused to offer any "premature" tally.

By the time Duncan told his supporters to go home, he'd resigned himself to losing.

After a sleepless night, the official tally put him behind by just ninety-eight votes. With write-in and absentee ballots still to be counted, an upset loomed tantalizingly close. He huddled with Kai, plotting strategy.

During the lull, Duncan would publicly express naive forbearance while Kai privately amplified the chaos, implanting stories in all the state's major dailies about the chicanery of the Machine. He told of unmonitored polling stations, corrupt committeemen, dumpsters filled with discarded ballots. Fortunately, the Better Governmental Association had chronicled it all with pictures and eyewitnesses.

Meanwhile, public sentiment built in their favor. True to his word, Jesse Jackson led protests daily, with PUSH adherents circling outside City Hall, waving placards and chanting slogans such as "Justice for all of us." Letters to the editor ran heavily in Duncan's favor. Congressmen and state representatives called for a federal inquiry. Even the League of Women Voters condemned the "appearance of impropriety."

Kai threatened that if all the irregularities were not corrected, they would sue for a statewide recount. They would camp out in the lobby of the election office. They would exercise the one power that remained to them: the power to complain. Even if it delayed the results for weeks, they would remain steadfast, demanding an end to the Chicago style.

Before they could deploy any of these stratagems, the governor called. He wanted a private meeting, somewhere outside the view of media or politicos, so they borrowed the Mirage.

Stratton arrived in a black sedan, escorted by a single unmarked police cruiser, and shuffled inside before anyone could identify him. There he eyed the place suspiciously, circling the table where Duncan sat and studying the dingy decor as though expecting to find a Nixon recorder.

Without provocation, the governor began a diatribe about the false accusations in the media. With his big body and booming courtroom voice, he took over the room. His manner was imperious, aloof, disdainful. He jabbed an oversized finger into the table, setting it off balance. His face reddened, his jaw clenched, and his muscles flexed as though he intended to rip from his suit, Hulk-like. He concluded with the charge, "Quit stirring skepticism about the state's electoral practices."

"We've only exposed the ugly truth," Duncan said.

To pacify his guest, Duncan poured a glass of sparkling water as the governor loomed over him. He recited the half dozen arguments Kai had listed. Fraud hurt the state, damaged its reputation, undermined public confidence. Every election would be tainted by its reach. All the while, Duncan ignored the awkwardness of appealing to his adversary for help.

The governor responded with another tirade, this time directed at Duncan's "selfishness." He lectured about the sacrifices of public service and "accepting the will of the people." He did all he could to intimidate his challenger into submission.

Throughout, Kai sat quiet, studying the governor until he paused to regain his breath. Then the advisor said, "No one benefits from the Machine's monopoly on power."

His statement spread through the room like steam from the hissing radiators, infusing every corner until no one could ignore its discomfort. Even Big Bill shed his coat and accepted a seat. He listened silently while Kai recounted all the elections that had been stolen in the past, including many statewide posts.

Meanwhile, Duncan studied his opponent. His suits came off the rack, and his haircut from the local barber, befitting his image as a man of the people. Deposed from the lectern, he more resembled a feeble grandfather, with thinning hair and straining vision. His expression softened to a resigned stare, and his big body slumped into the chair. Even he felt gelded by the Machine.

Prior to taking office, the governor built his reputation by prosecuting corrupt politicians. He'd put away his predecessor in the statehouse, Otto Kerner, as well as dozens of Daley's underlings. Yet throughout his years in the U.S. Attorney's office, the mayor had eluded his reach.

Still, Stratton promised vaguely to "investigate."

Instead, he ordered a recount of all the Machine's wards, overseen by state employees, who tossed thousands of fraudulent ballots. By the end of the cleansing, Duncan stood as the undisputed victor.

To celebrate, Duncan and Kai returned to the Mirage. Dusk had descended on the city, masking the bar's obvious flaws, while the clanging radiators provided a defense against the oncoming chill.

"I still don't know how we won," Duncan said to Pamela, who remained as barkeep, "but thanks." He raised a shot of single malt Scotch, which he'd brought himself, as toast.

"You should thank the state board of election," she said. "They made it happen."

"You mean Big Bill Stratton," Kai said. "He appointed half their members. They do his bidding."

Duncan downed the liquor, redolent and peaty, and chased it with a salty pretzel, then paused. "Why was he so keen to see me win?"

Silence followed as Pam refilled the pretzel bowl while Kai stared into the mirror behind her.

"He handpicked me," Duncan said.

Kai nodded.

"Why?"

"Doesn't matter. You won."

"Because he thinks I'll be easier to beat in the general?"

Kai shrugged and enjoyed another draught of the liquor.

"Meet the new boss, same as the old boss," Duncan said.

"Not once you unseat him."

"And how do we do that? He's got a machine of his own, only its gears turn statewide."

Kai shrugged and smiled. "By demanding an honest election."

About David Hagerty

David Hagerty's fiction is informed by his early career as a police reporter, and later as a teacher in the county jail. David's short stories are widely published, most recently in *Alfred Hitchcock's Mystery Magazine* and *Big Pulp*.

His debut novel, *They Tell Me You Are Wicked*, is inspired from the most infamous event in the history of his hometown: the real life killing of a political candidate's daughter. Book two in the series, *They Tell Me Your Are Crooked*, is set two years later, after the hero, Duncan Cochrane, has become governor. He's haunted by the family secret that got him elected and fighting a sniper who's targeting children in Chicago. In his latest book, *They Tell Me You Are Brutal*, Cochrane searches for a saboteur who is poisoning pain medications, all while trying to protect his family from personal and political ruin.

To find out more about David Hagerty, visit http://www.davidhagerty.net.

OPERATION FAIR VOTE

KRIS CALVIN

"SHE'S TOO CLEVER BY HALF."

Jolly said it with the good-natured grin that punctuated most of his comments and had resulted in his nickname years ago.

"Much too clever," Marco agreed. He used a biscuit to soak up the last of the sauce, all that remained on his plate of the chicken l'orange Jolly had prepared earlier in the day.

Emily was not fooled by her two fathers pretending they didn't notice her deep scowl. She knew they thought her theatrical but really, they gave her no choice. In three months, she would be 12 years old. She had to impose some order, some decorum on the household. The days when they could all behave as though they were small children were behind them.

Besides, Emily didn't believe there was such a thing as too clever.

At age six, given responsibility for rinsing the dishes before loading them into the dishwasher, she'd set them on the floor for Jasper, their aging Labrador, to do a preliminary cleaning. It would've been a great success if only Jasper hadn't attacked the task with such gusto that he later vomited profusely in Marco's study.

That was the first time Emily could remember Jolly happily commenting on her "excessive cleverness." His pronouncement this evening had followed her attempt to receive automated updates regarding the weather in Italy, where her best friend Simona had recently moved. Also, successful, if one didn't pay too much attention to the fact that her phone was now stubbornly communicating only in Italian.

The kitchen with its buttercup yellow walls and vintage white appliances felt bright and warm. Marco was busy brewing dark-roasted decaf for him and Jolly, and preparing steamed milk with a splash of coffee for Emily. Their ritual, handed down by Jolly's mother, of sipping after-dinner drinks from gold-rimmed china cups was important to her fathers. But as she covered the chicken she'd left uneaten, and pictured unwrapping it for lunch tomorrow at school, Emily felt butterflies in her stomach.

"I need to finish my algebra assignment," she said, knowing schoolwork was an acceptable reason for her to bow out. "Sorry, but I better take my coffee to my room."

Marco glanced at Jolly, and something seemed to pass between them. With a slight bow, Jolly pulled out an empty chair for Emily, like a maître d' in a formal restaurant.

"Sit, Madame," he said.

Marco added, "15 minutes, then you can get to work."

She was about to argue when Jolly disappeared into the pantry, emerging with a small, round cake decorated with the words "Congratulations, Emily" in bright blue icing on an ivory buttercream background.

She stepped back. She felt herself flush, making the freckles across her nose stand out.

What is wrong with them? she thought. *It's bad luck.*

Seeing her expression, Marco said, "We know your school elections aren't until tomorrow, Em. We just wanted . . ."

With a strained smile, Jolly broke in. "We just wanted to congratulate you on having made such an excellent choice of parents. If that's not worthy of celebration, I don't know what is."

Emily took in Marco's large, gentle face, concerned, and Jolly's sharper features, hopeful.

"All right, 15 minutes," she said firmly, sitting down.

She supposed a small slice of cake in advance of the vote, offered with such love, shouldn't jinx her chances of becoming 6th grade class president. Upon lifting her fork, taking a bite, and discovering it was moist, buttery and not-too-sweet, Emily decided it might even help.

Emily's bedroom, its walls a deep forest green, was part of an addition over the garage that included a bathroom and a small den/TV room that she never used. Her desk was centered beneath a large window that overlooked the street. She carefully set the china cup, filled with still-steaming hot milk, next to her algebra worksheet and sat down. Though the sun had set, she could just make out the silhouette of her school at the end of the block, illuminated by dim yellow lights.

Jolly had once told her that the quality of the schools in Taylor was the reason he and Marco bought the house in the small Northern California town seven years ago, when they'd decided they were ready for a child.

Ready, as it turned out, for her.

Her parents still both worked in downtown Sacramento, which meant a daily commute. Emily used to have a before-school sitter for the hour they were on the road, but when she turned eleven she insisted she was too old for that. Besides, she could see Maria, the crossing guard who arrived each day at 7:15 am, from her bedroom window—an adult was only a shout away. When her parents remained unconvinced, she called them upstairs one morning and demonstrated by screaming at the top of her lungs "Maria." Even with the window closed, Maria had turned her head towards the sound.

Despite this resulting in another "too clever" exclamation from Jolly, who had been standing right next to Emily, she was permitted her early morning independence.

Having double-checked each algebra answer, leaving nothing to chance, Emily opened a bright red folder she'd labeled "IMPORTANT" and removed her Taylor Middle School ballot. She laid it neatly on the desk, smoothing out the edges.

The school's Head Librarian, Ruth Hopper, in charge of student government, had explained in a notice sent home that the school took extremely seriously the need to have fair elections, and in particular, to prevent cheating. One year, a boy had picked up many blank ballots and stuffed the ballot box, voting for himself over and over. He was found out, but since then Librarian Hopper had devised a new system.

One official ballot was now issued to each student, who

was directed to sign it and mark the box next to their chosen candidate, using only blue or black ink. Ballots were submitted in the library, handed directly to Ms. Hopper, with a student observer present to check each voter's name off a master list. To limit the opportunities for monkey business, as Librarian Hopper called all inappropriate behavior, voting occurred strictly between 7:30 and 8:30 am on Election Day.

Tomorrow, Emily thought.

She looked at her ballot for what must've been the hundredth time.

Candidates for the Office of 6th Grade Class President
Select one:
___ *Dean Forrest*
___ *Emily Udovic-Jones*

She'd been waiting for the right moment to cast her vote. She wasn't sure why, but it hadn't come.

There was a soft knock on her door, followed by Jolly easing it open, a tray balanced on one hand.

"Protein—almonds," he said. "And brain food, sliced apples."

Emily didn't know what apples did for the brain, exactly, but food was Jolly's way of making everything all right. She moved her algebra paper aside to make space, and picked up her ballot to return it to the folder.

Noticing it in her hand, Jolly said, "You check that box right now, Ms. Emily Udovic-Jones, and put it in your backpack." He ruffled her short, red hair. "You wouldn't want to lose by one vote just because you left your ballot at home."

Emily responded with her trademarked scowl.

She was the most organized one in her family, there was no way she would forget to vote. Still, it had to be done, and she guessed there was no time like the present. She lifted her pen, made a large, clear "X" that filled the box next to her name, returned the paper to the folder and the folder to her backpack.

It did feel good, she realized.

After Jolly left, Emily gathered her pajamas to get ready for bed when she heard barking from Wyatt Miller's yard. Wyatt was in Emily's grade, though he had a different homeroom. She didn't really know him, he'd just moved next door with his mom the month before school started. He seemed quiet, she'd never heard him say more than a few words. But she had noticed he'd become best friends with Dean Forrest, her opponent for class president. The two boys both played on the basketball team.

The barking got louder, and she heard Wyatt trying to deal with it.

"Cosmo, shh, Cosmo come here!"

Wyatt's pug, Cosmo, didn't so much yap as emit a rolling, rumbling sound, more like a put-put car starting up in cold weather, or a turtle with a head cold, than what Emily would have expected from a dog, even from a very little one. Her Labrador, Jasper, passed a year after Emily arrived, but she remembered the deep, distinct barks he'd made.

She thought it was awfully late for Cosmo to be in the yard, though at night the time for his outdoor play did seem to vary. But each and every morning like clockwork, at seven-thirty she could hear Cosmo bark joyously, then Wyatt calling 15 minutes later for him to come in, not that it always worked. From the side window over her bed, she'd twice seen Wyatt chase Cosmo around the yard to get him back inside.

She turned over, but couldn't get to sleep. It was like

there was a neon sign in her brain flashing on and off "election tomorrow...election tomorrow."

She thought again about Wyatt and Dean, how she saw them together a lot, and realized Wyatt's was one vote Dean could count on, for sure. Even if Emily's ideas were better—a sister school in another country, ice cream sundaes in the cafeteria every Friday—she knew Wyatt wasn't going to consider what was best for the school, the way he was supposed to. His would just be a "Best Friend Vote."

Were Best Friend Votes fair? Emily wondered.

Usually, she concluded, *because each candidate's best friend would vote for them, and those votes would cancel each other out.*

But not this time.

Because her best friend, Simona, was gone.

She sat up and leaned against the headboard, too bothered to even think about sleeping. She recalled how Librarian Hopper kept saying that the most important thing about an election is it has to be fair.

But how can that be, Emily thought, *if one person's vote is never in question, never able to be won by the best candidate?* She realized, then, that Dean having Wyatt's vote was almost like the election was rigged against her from the beginning.

She knew she could stand losing, even by only one vote, but not if that vote wasn't a real one.

She wondered if there was anything she could do.

Wyatt called Cosmo one last time, and then it was, finally, blissfully, quiet.

And it came to her.

"Operation Fair Vote."

A little risky, to be sure, but it was the only way Emily could think of to right the wrong that would, otherwise, most certainly happen.

Her plan firmly in mind, she set the alarm on her phone to have an extra 15 minutes in the morning. Knowing it would wake her in Italian, she smiled, lay back down and soon fell fast asleep.

Emily could not believe how long it had taken her fathers to leave.

Marco couldn't find his trench coat. Jolly poured himself a second cup of coffee. Then, they'd both wanted to see how she was feeling, and to make sure that she understood, win or lose in the election, she was the most wonderful person in the world.

When at last they were gone, she grabbed the first belt she saw hanging in Marco's closet, thin and black with a silver buckle. She hoped it wasn't the most expensive, or the most dear to him.

Next, she hurried to the linen closet and chose a towel. Bath size, a dark color.

Lastly, a return to the kitchen. But as she went to get a small plastic bag from one of the drawers, she saw the time, and felt a surge of panic overtake her.

It was 7:24.

She threw herself at the refrigerator, yanked the door open, pulled the foil off last night's half-eaten chicken breast, then stuffed it directly in the pocket of her sweatshirt as she skidded out the back door.

Ducking behind a trashcan, she crouched low and listened.

She wrinkled her nose, the garbage smelled of the flounder Jolly had baked three nights ago. When she looked up, she saw thick, dark clouds that threatened rain.

Emily wished Simona was there, that she hadn't moved to Italy.

She couldn't tell which was faster, the beating of her heart as it raced, or her breathing, which she feared might cause her to hyperventilate. She closed her eyes, and forced herself to take a long slow intake of air as she reviewed her plan.

Each day, at 7:30 in the morning Wyatt Miller let Cosmo out in the backyard. 15 minutes later, Wyatt let him back in. Every day. Except once, when Cosmo had gotten out and Wyatt had to search the neighborhood to find him. Wyatt had missed first period at school. She'd heard him telling Dean at recess about how the back gate was left ajar by a workman. Wyatt had followed the road in front of their house to the dog park near the high school, where Cosmo was barking at the wire fence as though the dog owners inside were rude not to invite him in. It was the most Emily had ever heard Wyatt speak, and he didn't seem too bothered by what had happened, more like it was a funny story.

The sound of brief, rapid-fire barking made Emily jump, she knocked into a trashcan, almost tipping it over. After waiting a long minute and hearing no voices, she ran next door. She dropped the towel and the belt and looked for the latch to open the gate. With a sinking feeling, she saw there was none, it must only open from the inside. She stood on tiptoes and tried to reach over the top, but wasn't tall enough.

She thought hard, then turned and ran full speed to her house and grabbed the squat, metal stool they kept in the utility room off the kitchen. She tore back outside, set it flush against the gate and stepped up onto it. Stretching, she found she was just able to locate the interior latch and coax it open. She jumped off, pushed the stool aside and dropped to her knees, pulling the gate open an inch.

Stuffing her hand into her sweatshirt pocket, she tore bits of chicken off the deboned breast, sticky with orange sauce, then laid the meat flat on one palm, ready to hold it out for Cosmo.

Peeking through the gap in the gate, she saw him at the far side of the yard.

He was digging for something when he abruptly stiffened, brought his square, little head up, his smushed-in pug face and big, round eyes turned in her direction, and he charged towards her on his stumpy legs, barking furiously.

It belatedly occurred to Emily that Cosmo might not be a nice dog.

She fell back onto her rear, and was scooting away from him when he shot through the gate and jumped on her. In what felt like one swift motion he vacuumed the chicken off her hand, then dove for her face, licking it with his slobbery tongue.

She leaned back and tried to push him off of her when she realized with a start that her goal should be to hold onto him. She tried not to think about where his tongue had been before it made contact with her face as she looped an arm around his compact, barrel chest. He continued to lick her, his curly tail vibrating in what she guessed was his best effort at wagging it. She grabbed the towel with her free hand and threw it over him, then managed to get back onto her knees and to use the fence to steady herself to stand up. She glanced to be sure the gate was ajar and then stooped with the wriggling dog held tightly against her to pick up Jolly's belt. The idea she'd had to use it as a leash now seemed ridiculous.

She didn't have any hands left for the stool, so she kicked it in front of her as she focused on getting back to her house. She felt like she was in some kind of bizarre challenge, a dog-carrying, stool-kicking race, akin to ones she had to refused to run on the Fourth of July, carrying eggs or trapped in sacks.

Once inside, Cosmo seemed less interested in her face than her sweatshirt pocket, which still had chicken in it. She gave him a little piece, but was conscious of Jasper's upset tummy after eating human food, so she didn't want to give Cosmo too much. She ran upstairs with him still wrapped in the towel in her arms, which turned out to be a surprisingly effective way to carry a ten-pound dog, although she hoped she wouldn't have use for the technique ever again. She deposited him in the TV room, where she'd set a bowl of water the night before, and made sure the door was tightly closed. Only then did she take a breath and check the time.

7:44. What had seemed like an eternity to execute her mission had only been 14 minutes.

She raced into her bedroom, peeled off the chicken-filled sweatshirt, grabbed a fresh sweater and her backpack. She paused to be sure the folder was still inside and that the ballot was in the folder. All good. As she started down the stairs she listened for barking, but it was quiet. Maybe Cosmo appreciated being in the warm house, she thought, and he'd curled up for a nap.

She reminded herself that she would come back as soon as the election was over, during her study hall, and return Cosmo to his yard. No harm done. Operation Fair Vote would be complete, and the integrity of the Taylor Middle School 6th Grade Presidential Election, at least with respect to the Best Friend Vote, would be assured.

Librarian Hopper sat behind a gray folding table across

from the circulation desk. Seated next to her was a student Emily didn't recognize, he must be from one of the upper grades. Behind them hung a large banner that said, "Vote Here." A strip of wide yellow tape had been placed on the linoleum floor about six feet from the table. Written on it in black marker were the words "Wait Your Turn Behind This Line."

Emily joined the four students queued up behind the yellow line while a boy holding a skateboard under one arm cast his vote. The girl directly in front of Emily turned to her, smiling, and said, "I'm going to vote for you. I love your idea of a sister school in another country."

Emily thanked her, and for the first time since she'd conceived of Operation Fair Vote, remembered why she'd decided to run for class president. It was because she did have good ideas, and she wanted to help her school.

The line crept forward until it was Emily's turn.

She extended her ballot to Librarian Hopper, who made no attempt to take it. Emily knew the librarian well, but this morning the woman seemed to be all business.

"Please check your ballot carefully before you hand it in," Ms. Hopper said. "Be sure you've signed it and that you've indicated your preferred candidate. There are pens here if you need them."

Emily nodded. She was having difficulty finding her voice. While the student observer searched for her name on a long list, Emily checked the large, round clock on the wall over the circulation desk.

8:21. Only nine minutes left in the voting period.

Her ballot successfully processed, she found an empty table along the wall to the left of the fiction section.

She was glad it wouldn't be long until she could go home and return Cosmo to Wyatt. It made her uncomfortable when she thought about the lie she planned to tell him, that she'd found the dog running loose up the block. But the important thing was that Cosmo was fine, Wyatt would be fine, and the election would be fair, just like Ms. Hopper said it had to be. Still, the butterflies in Emily's stomach from last night seemed to have been replaced by bees. She felt a little bit sick. Thinking a distraction might help, she got up and went to a nearby display of books on elections. As she was looking at the titles, she saw Dean Forrest, her opponent, coming through the double glass doors into the library. He was tall, with long arms and legs, no surprise that he was on the basketball team. When he saw her, he raised his hand halfway in greeting and she did the same.

She had first period free, study hall, but she realized they must have called Dean out of class. She looked over and saw that Librarian Hopper and her sidekick were no longer at the voting table. They had to be in the back office tallying the results, and would be out soon to tell them who won.

Dean had gone to sit at the table where she had been, setting his backpack next to hers. She was about to join him when she heard a pattering sound from the front entrance to the building. Slowly at first, then faster, it had started to rain. Through the glass doors, she could see fat, heavy drops falling, one by one, gathering strength, making the concrete walkway appear slick and dark.

Emily felt stricken.

She was sure her face had paled.

Wyatt must've made it to the dog park by now, and turned back. What would he do, thinking Cosmo was caught out in the rain?

Would he call his mother? She worked in the city, like

Emily's parents. It would take her at least an hour to get back, maybe longer. Or would Wyatt keep looking on his own, calling out as he got soaked and maybe shivered in the cold? Worst of all, would he go past the boundaries of their neighborhood, beyond the dog park? Get lost or hit by a car that didn't see him as the rain came down?

Emily couldn't sit there any more, she knew what she had to do. But as she went to retrieve her backpack, she saw someone running towards the library entrance in a yellow slicker with a hood, his head down against the now-driving rain. He pushed the door open and rushed inside.

It was Wyatt.

He looked towards the empty table with the banner "Vote Here" still hanging above it, then turned towards the circulation desk. He was red in the face, and when he pushed his hood back, his hair was plastered against his head. He pulled a folded paper from his pocket. He spoke to a student assistant behind the counter, gesturing and looking more upset by the minute. He assistant nodded, left through the door to the office in the back, and returned with Librarian Hopper.

Wyatt said something to her.

Ms. Hopper shook her head, as she gestured to the clock on the wall.

Wyatt stepped back, his shoulders slumped. He walked slowly to the waste can by the front door, tore the paper he was holding in half, and dropped it in the trash before leaving the building.

Emily was frozen in her seat, staring after him, when Librarian Hopper approached the table where she and Dean sat, and joined them.

"You have been excellent candidates, conducting yourself well with positive campaigns. I want to compliment you, "she said. "The votes have been tallied, with a student witness present. It is my duty to tell you the official results. We are completely transparent here, so I will give you the totals." Her voice softened. "This is where you truly show your character, how you behave in victory and defeat." She looked pointedly from Dean to Emily. "To you, at 11 or 12 years old, that may sound silly. But it is important." Then she looked again at Dean. "Congratulations, Dean you are the new Taylor Middle School 6th Grade Class President."

Dean burst into a smile and started to pump his fist, but then pulled his arm down and looked towards Emily.

"Emily, you put forth an admirable effort. You gained only one vote less than Dean. I hope you will choose to run again next semester."

Emily's eyes widened.

It couldn't be.

One vote.

She'd lost by one vote.

It hadn't been a Best Friend's Vote, she thought, and her mind turned again to Wyatt.

"Thank you, Ms. Hopper. Thank you, Dean. I mean, congratulations, Dean," she said in a rush as she grabbed her backpack, jumped up and headed to the door, leaving Dean open-mouthed and Ms. Hopper frowning, looking concerned.

As Emily passed the waste can, she slowed, noticing Wyatt's torn paper on top inside. She looked behind her. Dean was surrounded by people congratulating him, Librarian Hopper had gone behind the desk. Emily reached in and pulled out the paper. She looked at it, then dropped it back in the can, and went to find Wyatt.

When she got outside, the rain had lightened. She saw

him coming out of a classroom, the yellow slicker hard to miss. He broke away from the other kids and jogged across the grass in her direction.

Emily could feel her heart pounding again, she wanted desperately to prepare herself for whatever it was he might say, but she couldn't imagine what that might be.

Then she saw that Wyatt was smiling at her.

"Thank you so much for saving Cosmo," he said. "Where did you find him?"

Emily squinted as she looked at Wyatt, as though she must be seeing things. She bit her lip. If her parents were there they would say she was being theatrical, but really, she had no idea what was going on.

"I saw him jumping up and down on the back of the sofa, in that room, above the garage. Your room? Anyway, he was barking like crazy. When you came to my house to tell me, I must have already been out looking for him, and I know you had to go to school for the election and everything."

Emily got it, the version of events Wyatt had constructed from the facts as he saw them. The one where she had saved, instead of kidnapped Cosmo, and stopped at Wyatt's house to tell him, rather than going straight to school and hoping Wyatt would miss the vote.

She still didn't know what to say to him, but, fortunately, Wyatt wasn't done. "I really liked your ideas," he said. "Ice cream every Friday, even when it's cold."

Emily had seen his ballot.

He wasn't lying. He had marked her name for class president.

"But Dean's your best friend." She had to ask. "Doesn't he automatically get the Best Friend Vote?"

Wyatt shook his head. "I've never heard of that." He

cleared his throat and added, "I've got to get to class. Do you want to meet at break and go get Cosmo? I mean, together? I hope he's not doing any damage to your room or anything."

She nodded and watched him jog back across the lawn.

Too clever, she thought. *It might be true, I might be too clever by half.*

Still, maybe not too clever to learn.

About Kris Calvin

Kris Calvin is a past local elected official who knows politics from the inside out. She's been honored for her advocacy on behalf of children by the California State Assembly and the California Governor's Office. Kris' education includes degrees from Stanford and UC Berkeley with training in economics and forensic psychology.

More than a decade of work with state legislators and bureaucrats provides Kris with ample fodder for murder and mayhem in her debut Sacramento-based mystery series, which features lobbyist Maren Kane as an amateur sleuth. Kris' novel *One Murder More* won the 2016 Silver Falchion Awards for Best Fiction First Novel, Best Mystery/ Crime, and the Judge's Awards for both Political Thriller and Detective/Women Sleuths.

To learn more about Kris Calvin, visit http:// www.kriscalvin.com.

Civic Duty

CAMILLE MINICHINO

BOO NELSON COUNTED AT LEAST twenty-five guys ahead of him, a few women, too. Probably the same number behind him. He didn't think there'd be so many lined up for this deal. Ten bucks for what they were calling a training session. Jury duty paid more and all you did was sit around in case your name was called. But then there was that promised one hundred dollars on the actual day of work, whatever that was.

"I'm freezing," Boo told the guy in front of him, who was dressed like most of the men, in worn jeans and a fake leather jacket. The dude had a serious spider web tattoo, partly visible behind his ear, above his upturned collar.

"Yeah, they're supposed to open the building at ten, but"—Spiderweb Man looked at his cellphone—"it's ten twelve."

Smartphones—they made everyone seem on top of things, right to the minute.

Boo shifted his weight from one leg to the other and back, joining the out-of-sync chorus line trying to keep from becoming ice sculptures. They waited outside the decaying building, one in a row of what must have been busy warehouses in better days.

The ad had said *Workers Wanted. One day only. November 6 for cleanup project.* The job was two weeks away. The fine print gave this address for today's training session.

Boo thought it was a little strange, planning a cleanup two weeks ahead of time, needing what? Some kind of certificate? Halloween was one week away. Was that the project? "Maybe they're going to hand out those trash picker poles so we can stab candy wrappers from trick or treaters," Boo said.

Spiderweb Man laughed. "How do they know how much mess there'll be or where it'll be?"

"Not our problem," Boo said, to an "Amen" from Spiderweb Man and others around them.

One thing for sure, a sawbuck in the hand was worth...more than zero, which is what Boo had been earning ever since his old boss caught him pocketing money from the tip jar. As if food truck customers were big tippers. Not in that neighborhood. Boo shuffled his feet, aggravated at the memory. He ought to report the old bastard for the rotten crap he passed off as meat. It tasted like—

"What do you think this job is, really?" Spiderweb Man asked.

"We're about to find out," a woman behind him said, as a loud screeching sound signaled the opening of the enormous metal door that reached halfway up the gray building. Boo turned to see a woman old enough to be his mother, assuming she'd had him as a teenager, like his real mother did. Was Ma better off dead now, rather than out here in the cold looking for a lousy few bucks? Boo had half a mind to split, to cruise the boulevard instead, and look for NOW HIRING signs. Oh, wait—he screwed up his mouth and kicked a piece of gravel to the curb—he'd already done that.

Boo zipped his jacket all the way up as if he were walking into a storm instead of into a building. He rubbed his hands together, making the hole in his old knit gloves even bigger. He wondered how much a new pair would cost. He headed for the door, between Spiderweb Man and his mother look-alike.

Bare concrete floor and walls, rows of folding chairs, exposed pipes and wires, coffee and donuts on a rickety picnic table.

"Hey, what is this?" Spiderweb Man asked. "Smell that burnt java? Are they tricking us into an AA meeting?" The guy looked peeved, but he rushed the donut table along with Boo and everyone else.

Boo took a seat at the end of a back row, in case he decided to make a quick exit.

Once everyone got settled with breakfast—a donut in their hands, another in a napkin on their laps—a tall trim guy, dressed better than any of them, appeared at the front of the room. He pulled a large blank whiteboard from behind a canvas curtain and set it next to a podium.

Boo watched as the dude brushed some invisible speck off his shoulders. The guy's haircut alone must have cost three figures. Probably part of some ritzy spa day, like where Boo had that valet parking job. Until they caught him in the glove compartment of a brand new Jag. Not *in* the glove compartment, Boo corrected himself. He laughed, then quickly cleared his throat to cover up the sound before anyone thought he was nuts.

"Ladies and gentlemen," the stiff white boss at the podium said, in a way that told Boo he considered his audience anything but. "Let's get started. I'm Jim." *Sure you are*, Boo thought. *No way do you want us to be able to find you again.* Boo figured his name was something like Walker or Spencer the third. Something rich.

I should talk, Boo murmured. Stuck with some famous black brother's name from a hundred years ago.

"I'll be running down the list of things we're going to want you to do on November 6," Jim said. "But first, I need to be sure—"

A hand shot up in the first row. The woman Boo now considered his mother had a question. "That's voting day, right?"

So-called Jim pointed his marker at Mom and smiled. "You bet. A very important day, and that's why we're here. We want things to go as smoothly as possible. I'm going to start with a few things you can do to help."

Jim explained that the job was to make people who were waiting in line to vote feel comfortable abandoning that meaningless chore. "There are so many other things they can do besides"—he threw out a loud, annoyed breath —"stand in a long line, explain who they are, listen to some garbled instructions, yada yada, and in the end"—another heavy breath—"what does it matter who they vote for?" He paused, winding up for the punch line. "The government gets in either way."

A few snickers, but mostly it was Jim's laughter that

echoed through the hall. He stepped over to the whiteboard and flipped it to reveal a numbered list.

Boo squinted and caught the first few items.

1. *Freezing.*
2. *Back problems.*
3. *ID.*

Jim pointed to the board. "Here are some ways you can ease the burden of the potential voters. First, we know it's bound to be cold that day, so you approach a guy and sympathize. 'Aren't you freezing?' you might ask. 'Why don't you split and get some coffee? This line isn't going away.'" Jim paused, took a swig from a water bottle on the podium. "Same with number two there. You see a guy bending over, flexing his knees or something. You say, 'Hey, it's pretty tough on the joints, huh? It's not exactly worth it, is it?' Or you see a woman with a kid . . ."

Jim's voice drifted off, like Boo's attention. Boo slunk down in the metal chair and folded his arms across his chest. Not too comfortable, but Jim's droning would help him catch a few z's.

He got the point. Walk along the line, act real friendly, and try to get the mark to leave. He watched enough news to know that this neighborhood was mostly blue collar. Like him, when he had a collar.

Boo lifted the hood of his sweatshirt and ran his hands through tight black curls, badly in need of a trim. He replaced his hood and slumped farther down in the chair. He came to when Spiderweb Man, in the next seat, nudged him.

"Hey, man, he's almost done and he's going to give out assignments. And our ten bucks."

"Thanks, Bro. I miss anything?" Boo asked.

"Yeah, don't carry a sign or a gun. It's illegal."

"Got it."

Job day. By noon on November 6, Boo had managed to coax only a half dozen people to leave, and that was mostly because of the unruly group chanting at the edges of the parking lot.

Spiderweb Man had warned Boo that Big Brother would be watching on voting day—no pay without a good report. Unmarked cars would be patrolling the area, making sure the workers were doing their jobs.

Boo had seen at least two cars he fingered for the fleet. He didn't know if there was a quota, like the cops had. Which was why they were always on him about something, by the way. Now how many people was he supposed to talk out of voting?

Boo was starving. He wished he'd stayed awake during fake Jim's talk long enough to ask about a lunch break. He wondered if there was a vending machine inside the polling place, an old church hall, slightly more appealing than the battered warehouses a few blocks away. He headed for the doorway, searching the line of people for maybe one more easy target. He'd learned that if a woman kicked off a shoe, in spite of the cold, that was a sign her feet were killing her and she was ready to leave. Or if a guy checked his watch every few minutes—another sign—he could easily be talked out of waiting around to mark a ballot.

Boo cruised the line. A few yards from the entrance, he saw a woman who looked familiar. Not mom-familiar this time, but teacher-familiar.

"Boo? Booker T. Nelson, is that you?"

The voice was familiar, too. Boo was startled, unprepared to meet anyone he knew, let alone someone from his not-entirely-honorable youth.

"Miss Andrews? Hey." Boo stuck out his hand, then, on second thought, worried that it was disrespectful, not to mention it was wrapped in a dirty glove, and made a move to pull it back.

Too late. The very short Miss Andrews grasped his hand with one of hers and used the other to pat his holey glove.

Boo continued, looking down at her. "Yeah, I can't believe you remember me. High school was a long time ago."

"Yes, a long time ago. I'm retired now." She gave his hand a squeeze before letting go. "How could I forget you, Boo?"

For a minute Boo was afraid she was going to remind him of what a troublemaker he'd been. Or worse, of the days he'd shown up at school weak from hunger, all the times she'd pretended she'd mistakenly brought too much lunch and slipped him a sandwich.

But Miss Andrews had a different memory to share. "Not one of my other freshmen ever climbed between the top of the cabinets and the ceiling in my science classroom." She laughed, shaking her head. "Why was that again, Boo?"

Boo had a feeling she remembered why, but he shuffled his feet in an aw-shucks way and answered anyway, like the good student he never was. "I wanted to have the longest swinging pendulum in the class."

Miss Andrews nodded. "You were one of my most creative students, Boo."

Boo felt his face heat up in spite of the cold. He hoped his old teacher couldn't tell how uncreative he'd gotten since those days. And what would she say if she knew what he was doing here? Not that he was stealing or anything. Except he was. Stealing votes. Some cleanup project. Clean up the messy voters. He saw one of those unmarked cars go by, checking his progress getting rid of trash. His hands were stuffed in his pockets, so the driver didn't see Boo's middle finger.

He wondered if there was still time to shape up, maybe even get creative again with his life. Go back to those classes where you could get a certificate to do something useful. He'd always been pretty good at fixing things. Maybe—

"Say, Boo, would you like to grab a cup of coffee?" Miss Andrews interrupted his rambling mind. "Talk about old times?"

"Cool, Miss Andrews." Boo swallowed hard. "Don't you want to vote first?"

Miss Andrews waved her hand in front of her face. "Oh, I already voted."

"What? Then why are you in line?"

Miss Andrews reached up to whisper in Boo's ear. "I've actually been working, sort of." She plopped down off her tiptoes and put her arm through Boo's as they walked toward the coffee shop. "Not getting paid or anything," she continued. "I signed up to hang around a polling place and ferret out those people who try to stop folks from voting, from doing their civic duty. Do you know, in some places they close the polls early, without warning? They say the power went out or something. Or they say only property owners can vote. Or you need several forms of ID. One year I remember, they sent people . . ."

Boo had that drifting off problem, the way his mind wandered when people went on and on and he already got the point. He tuned in again to hear Miss Andrews end with "Aren't they just awful, Boo? Keeping people from their civic duty?"

Boo nodded. "They sure are, Miss Andrews. They sure are."

Author's Note

Booker T. "Boo" Nelson is a fictional character, but his day at the polls is, sadly, based on fact. States across the country have passed measures to make it harder for Americans in certain neighborhoods to exercise their fundamental right to vote. Other tactics, besides the one portrayed in Civic Duty, have also been used, like closing polling places early or moving them across town at the last minute, claiming power outages or lack of supplies. We hope that continued vigilance, advocacy, and litigation will rid the country of these methods of voter suppression once and for all.

About Camille Minichino

Camille received her Ph.D. in physics from Fordham University, New York City. She is currently on the faculty of Golden Gate University, San Francisco and teaches writing throughout the Bay Area. Camille is Past President and a member of NorCal Mystery Writers of America, NorCal Sisters in Crime, and the California Writers Club.

Camille has published over 20 novels and many short stories and nonfiction articles.

As **Camille Minichino**, she's published Periodic Table Mysteries, featuring retired physicist Gloria Lamerino.

As **Margaret Grace**, she writes the Miniature Mysteries, featuring miniaturist Geraldine Porter and her 11-year-old granddaughter, Maddie. The 9th in the series, *Matrimony In Miniature* was released in September 2016.

As **Ada Madison**, she's published the Professor Sophie Knowles Mysteries, featuring college professor Sophie Knowles.

As **Jean Flowers**, Camille writes The Postmistress Mysteries. The third in the series, *Addressed To Kill*, was released in July 2017.

To find out more about Camille Minichino, visit http://www.minichino.com and http://minichino.com/wordpress/.

Momma's Ballots

Derek Marsh, Jr.

Earl felt the sun's heat on his neck and tugged his moist collar closer for protection. The long walk from the bus stop to his daddy's fading ranch pushed him farther from a thankful mood with every step. This Thanksgiving Day was hotter than any Earl could remember.

He lived in an old ramshackle building converted into mean, small apartments right by a freeway entrance on the edge of East Bakersfield. His useless old man held on to life and their family home, nestled in the cheaper end of Panorama Boulevard, not the rich end that overlooked a broad stretch of the Kern River. No, his view had always been the flat, ugly town of Oildale below them, past the cliffs.

As a kid, riding his bike along the wide sidewalks had

been fun. As an adult with no bike or car or horse, he felt the eyes of richer people staring at him whenever he was outside. With nothing but bus fare, and not even always that, Earl felt exposed. When he finally spied the old house, the only one on the block in need of a paint job and a good weed-whacking, he cheered up a little. There'd be Budweiser and Boston Market for Thanksgiving dinner, at least.

A vision of his mother fluttered at the corner of Earl's vision as he walked up the cracked concrete steps. She had always greet him with a warm hug and a look into his eyes, a searching "how are you really?" sort of thing. Gone nearly a year now, Earl hoped to skip Thanksgiving entirely but his sister, newly skinny from a flirtation with meth, had begged him to join her and their father. He knew well enough that the old man would light into one of them at some point, and her odds were better if there were the two of them to choose from.

He let the screen door bang behind him, mostly to irritate his father, and headed straight for the fridge. "Happy Thanksgiving, Pop!"

The TV, screeching about something, was the only reply. Earl had hocked his own TV in a particularly bad month, so he settled into Momma's empty Barcalounger next to his father, and let the cool shade of the living room soothe him.

"Those people should spend less time complaining and more time working!" Pop said back to the pretty blonde lady on the television. She was showing a video of a black family in Flint, Michigan, pouring water into pans from bottles.

"Pop, I can't find a damn job this whole year, and not for lack of trying!" Earl took a thirsty swig from his Bud can for emphasis.

"You never did care for work." Pop's tone was dismissive. He stared at the television.

"You just like her legs, Pop."

Earl hoisted himself out of the Barcalounger and went looking for his sister. He found her in Pop's bedroom. She was sorting through their mother's clothing; well-preserved dresses and shoes from decades before, and purses that had been carved out of cows long before they put foreign names in gold and charged a fortune for them.

Earl said, "Damn, Sis, he still has all her stuff?"

"Sh! It took me months to get permission to tackle her half of the closet." Meg stopped long enough to give Earl a quick peck on the cheek. Her skin looked good again. He hoped she would stay away from that meth crowd for good this time.

Meg moved swiftly, like one of the ladies in the local JC Penney, sorting things into neat piles on the bed.

She said, "This here is just to give away. Don't nobody like the scratch of polyester on their skin anymore. These here are quality things—I don't really remember Mamma ever wearing them, do you?" Meg cocked her head, lost in thought.

Earl heard his own breathing and the screech of the TV as he gulped, trying to think of an answer.

At last he croaked, "Don't worry about that. You were little. That was back when The Men came around a lot." Earl feigned interest in the quality pile to distract his sister.

"I know all about Mamma's special friend. She told me in the hospital before she died. So she got these things from him?"

Earl felt stung. He had seen Momma go out with a man behind Pop's back when he was a child, when Meg was too small to remember, but Momma had never told him anything.

"Pop doesn't know. I thought you knew." Meg patted Earl's cheek and went back to sorting Momma's side of the closet.

Earl snorted. "My ass he didn't know. You were little, you don't remember how bad things got."

Meg tilted her head at him. "Were they ever good?"

Earl felt a little something give in his heart as he realized they really hadn't ever been good. And now his father was clinging to life, hoarding the house and threatening at least twice a year to cut Earl off entirely. Anger churned his stomach and made him want to break something.

As Meg hummed and sorted, and the TV blared from down the hall, he sauntered over to the tall Chesterfield with the little mirror on top and started slowly pulling open drawers.

"Stop it, Earl! You'll give Pop a heart attack!" Meg dropped Momma's clothes and pulled him away from the drawers. Earl had been sort of playing around, but also wondering if Pop still had that gun. He'd seen a glimpse of flat black metal toward the back of the top drawer once when he was a teen, before Pop had thrown him out of the room. Probably rusted by now, thought Earl. Probably not worth taking to the pawn shop.

"He's going to outlive us both." Earl whispered it as he let Meg lead him away from the Chesterfield.

"That's no way to think on Thanksgiving." Meg went back to sorting clothes and handbags and shoes, her slender back stiff, telling Earl he'd crossed a line.

"You gonna sell her good stuff?" Earl imagined a few twenties would help him survive until Christmas. Earl was glad Meg was doing it—he couldn't tell shit from shinola in the ladies wardrobe department.

"Depends on Pop."

Earl wanted his sister to turn around, to like him again. "Hey, Meg, you know who The Men were?"

She turned around, half-smiling. The Men, wearing suits and crisp shirts with ties pulled open a bit at the top, used to drop by their house. Sometimes they had a candy or toy for him or Meg.

"Momma didn't tell you who they were?" Earl felt a little ashamed that he hoped he knew something Meg didn't.

She shook her head.

"The Bakersfield Five. They used to come around here and treat Pop like he was one of them. Sort of."

Meg looked at him in disbelief. "That's just a dumb rumor. This town wasn't run in secret by five crackers. It got fucked up from everyday inertia and greed. Like everything always does."

Earl shook his head. "You ever wonder what Pops actually did for a living? You ever wonder how a guy who does 'odd jobs' bought a house on Panorama?"

"I thought the money came from Momma's relatives."

Earl stood close to her and spoke quietly, as if they were still little and their father could beat them if he caught them. "A kid, Ricky Morales, you remember him? He was crying on the playground and he looked at me and said my daddy called the Immigration on his daddy and he hated me. He was so little and skinny, I didn't even hit him for saying that. But it's true. Pops did odd jobs for the Bakersfield Five."

Meg stared at Earl. "Ricky had to leave school when they took his dad. I think they had to go back to Mexico. I never heard from him again." She looked so sad—it never occurred to him that Meg had known the little boy. He was probably in her class.

He kept going, feeling so proud of knowing something true and secret. "It's true. Those men would drop by to give him his orders. Remember how we weren't allowed to hang out in the kitchen when they were over? Even Momma couldn't be there except to deliver beers."

"I thought it was because they were swearing." Meg shook her head, disgust spreading across her plain features.

Earl spied an old banker's box on his father's side of the closet, pushed to the back. He listened: he heard nothing but the shrill chatter from Pop's TV. He dove for the banker's box and pulled it out, dropped it on the bed with a satisfied grunt.

Meg grabbed his hands before he could pull the faded lid off the top.

"Don't! He'll come in here and find us!"

"And what? We're grown-ass people. And he owes us— we're his kids." Earl hoped the box held something valuable, something he could sneak back in and steal. He was damn tired of waiting for Pops to die.

With Meg still trying to restrain him, Earl knocked the flimsy lid off. With a puff of dust, a few pieces of paper flew out of the box. Earl dug around frantically, looking for something like stocks or bonds, even though he wasn't exactly sure what they looked like. But he knew they didn't look like the papers in the box.

"Ballots?" Meg pulled a few out and looked at them. "Jesus Christ."

Curious, Earl looked at the paper nearest him. An election ballot, marked for Franklin Sperry. He looked at another. They were all ballots for Franklin Sperry for Supervisor.

"Earl. The man who gave Momma nice clothes. The

man she fell for, his name was Franklin."

The floor creaked and a shadow fell across the bed from the hallway. Earl and Meg jerked back from the bed as if it had grown red hot.

"You two ungrateful worms put that box back and get the hell out of my house." Pops stood in the doorway, rigid with anger.

Earl had been looking for something valuable so hard that he hadn't heard the TV turn off or Pops pad down the hall—two sounds he'd grown up dreading.

Pops said, "Go on., you greedy little shits. And take Momma's clothes with you if you want them so bad. But put that box back in the closet right now.

Meg shrank back from Pops, behind Earl.

"Not until you tell us why the hell you have a closet full of voter's ballots." Earl couldn't remember ever speaking to his father like that before. He suddenly felt clean and strong.

"I will not sully your Mother's memory with her one mistake. She let Franklin Sperry turn her head. When he lost that election she saw who was the real deal." Pop crossed his arms.

Earl stood his ground. "You mean she let you shame her into giving up on him."

He dropped the ballots but moved toward his father instead of putting the box back in the closet.

Meg whispered, "Daddy, she loved him."

A thought hit Earl so hard it made him want to throw up. Rage gripped him and forced the words out of his throat. "If you hadn't rigged an election, cuz that's what this is, she could have run off and married Franklin Sperry and we could have been his kids instead of yours and I wouldn't be living with field hands and hookers out in East

Bakersfield. You screwed us all over, you hateful miserable bastard!"

Pops eyes bulged for just a second, then he ran for the Chesterfield faster than Earl thought an old man could move. He pulled open the top drawer, and before Earl even saw it, he knew it was the gun.

Earl leapt across the bed to stop his father.

Behind him, Earl heard Meg screaming and running out of the room. He was too busy wrestling his wiry father's arms for the gun.

The two men fell.

Earl stood first, holding the gun with two hands, his arms rigid, pointing at his father.

"How could you? You ruined all our lives. Just so you could feel like a big man?"

Pops rose slowly, rubbing his bad hip. "I kept you all fed and clothed and educated. You have no right to judge me."

"What was it like, being married to a woman who hated you? How dare you judge me and my life when you did *this*?" Earl used the gun to point at the ballot box, crushed and spilling ballots all over the bed. "You threw an election, you sanctimonious old bastard. Lording this house over me during all my bad days, pretending to be better than you are."

"Shut up!" His father moved slowly toward Earl, who pointed the gun back at his father.

Earl moved closer to his father, barely able to see, willing his finger to stay loose on the trigger. "You stole a life from me and Momma and Meg. She does meth to feel *good enough*, you evil shit. I can't drink enough whiskey to feel *good enough*. You should be in jail and so should your rich friends that don't come around anymore."

Pops stepped slowly and carefully toward Earl, his hand

out for the gun.

Earl wouldn't back up. He jutted the gun toward his father to make him stop coming.

Pops stopped inches from the barrel. "Give. Me. My. Goddamned. Gun."

The decision to shoot came so fast, Earl didn't realize he'd pulled the trigger until his ears hurt from the loud sound in the small room. His father, suddenly bloody, fell to the floor. A weird gasp escaped Pops, and then there was no sound or movement at all.

The smell sickened Earl.

He held on to the gun a long moment before he left the bedroom. He saw his sister on the phone, but his ears were ringing and he couldn't quite hear what she was saying. She shrank behind the Barcalounger, phone in hand, as he passed by on his way to the kitchen.

"Don't worry, Meg."

Earl knew he had a minute or two to drink some of Pop's good whiskey before the cops could arrive. He leaned over the Barcalounger to look at Meg, who dropped the phone mid-sentence, her eyes wide.

Feeling lighter than he ever had, he said, "You sell this house and go someplace nice. Morro Bay, maybe? Someplace cool and clean. Promise me?" He smiled, hoping Meg would stay off the meth and have a happy life. Then he opened Pop's liquor cabinet and took a deep draw of whiskey straight from the bottle.

As the ringing in his ears stopped, Earl heard sirens in the dry autumn air as they came closer to the house. He set down the bottle and fired the gun one last time.

About Derek Marsh, Jr.

Derek Marsh is a writer of mystery. With no website, this editor's only clues to his existence are a Twitter handle, DerekMarshJr, which proclaims him an assistant to fabulous writers, and the address where we sent the check. Rumors abound about Derek Marsh, Jr.: retired English professor earning coffee money, a student who is on the eight-year plan, or even a fevered figment of a famous writer's imagination. Whomever Derek turns out to really be, we thank him for this story.

Another Statistic

Travis Richardson

Today is your last day on earth, but you don't know it. Tomorrow you'll be an obituary announcement. A victim in a police officer involved shooting. Another statistic.

Your death will cause a riot in Pinewood, North Carolina and a march in Raleigh. The Black Lives Matter movement will resurge, led by law student and future lawmaker, Tanya Coleman. The criminal trial will be watched by a breathless nation. When it ends with a hung jury for the officer, protests will erupt in major cities. And you'll remain an aching, infinite hole in your parents' hearts whose absence they'll never be able to fill.

But when you wake up early—four AM early—on a Tuesday, you question your sanity. Is it worth it? What difference can you really make? Isn't sleep more important?

It doesn't help that your roommate Ronald snores like a locomotive, oblivious to the world. He carries that obliviousness with him during his waking days too. Makes for an easier life, no doubt. Even when everything around you is being taken away and ground up into trash. Just ignore and consume. The American way. You wish you were less aware and could get a few more hours of sleep. It's not like they are paying you anything.

"Come on, man. Don't think like that," you mutter as you stumble into the bathroom.

After showering, you towel off and procure a Red Bull from the mini-fridge. Need some energy for the long day ahead. Ten minutes later you're out of the dorm, toothpaste-minty breath clinging to the air as you start up your ten-year-old Camry. Not flashy, but dependable. Kind of like you, right?

Google Maps says it will take you two hours and forty-five minutes to get to Pinewood. Right at seven AM on the dot if you do it right. Dependable Seth Anderson here, at your service.

The drive is boring with sixteen wheelers chugging west in the dark on Interstate 40 and 85. Kendrick Lamar, Rhianna, Drake, and Foo Fighters blast on your speakers. It's the road trip playlist you made for your cross-country trip two years ago. The Foos are a guilty pleasure you don't tell anybody about. As the sun begins to crest in the east, more civilian cars and trucks merge onto the highway.

It's seven when you park at the Pinewood Community Action Network. P-CAN for short. You blow warm breath on your knuckles and knock twice on the bright yellow door.

A heavy man with a shaved head and gray beard opens the door. Looks like he could have been a bouncer before calories took over.

"You the college boy to come and help us?" he says, looking a bit skeptical.

You feel the urge to tell him to shove it, but instead you nod and mumble, "Yes, sir."

A big grin creases his mouth. "Come on in," he says, throwing a heavy arm around your shoulder and leading you inside. "I'm Morgan."

The center is mostly a wide-open room with about fifty folding chairs and an elevated stage. Portraits of Dr. King, the Obamas, Maya Angelou, and other prominent black leaders hang on the walls. On one side of the room are a couple of folding tables with papers and a television playing the local Charlotte CBS morning news. A woman in her sixties walks up and shakes your hand. Her name is Clarice, and she tells you to "get some coffee and goodies over yonder."

You look across the room to another table, and that is when you see her: a woman of exquisite beauty about your age. Her face is framed perfectly by long cascading black curls as she takes a bite of a bear claw. Before you know what you're doing, you stride over, hand outstretched.

"Hello, I'm Seth."

She smiles as she chews, pointing at her mouth and then her glazed covered fingers holding the donut.

"Want a napkin?"

She nods.

You grab a handful and hand them over. "Coffee too?"

"Yes, please," she says with her mouth half full.

You grab a coffee pot and pour into two Styrofoam cups. "How do you like it?"

"Black's fine."

"Strong and black. Just like my warrior princess."

Morgan says with a thunderous laugh.

Clarice bops him on the head with a stack of flyers.

"What?" he asks.

"You're embarrassing the girl," Clarice says in a loud whisper.

The girl rolls her eyes like she's been through this routine before and grabs the coffee from your hand. After a sip she says, "Hello, I'm Tanya. Morgan's my goofball uncle."

"You in school?"

"Wake Forrest. Pre-law. You?"

"UNC. Engineering."

"Say what?" Morgan bellows. "A brother in the sciences. My mind is blown." He imitates his head exploding with his hands and requisite sound effects.

Tanya shakes her head again with dimples showing. It looks like she's blushing a little. Her eyes also glow as she studies you. "How come you came all the way out to Pinewood?"

"There was a call at the Black Student Association to help out in districts lacking...Um...resources. Not all of us have cars so I thought I'd come out here. You know, make a sacrifice. And yourself?"

"Uncle Morgan's trying to make a difference here. He's been rallying the black folks in the area to see if we can make an impact in spite of the odds."

"Crazy odds given the way Pinewood is split up."

Tanya nods her head. "But somebody's got to fight the good fight."

Pinewood has three US Congressional Districts running through it, which is nuts for a town with a population of 36,000. But with a forty percent black population and Hispanics edging close to ten, the Republicans in Raleigh made sure a razor-thin slice of a hundred-plus-mile-long

12th district minority-majority ran through Pinewood segmenting the minority vote with the two districts on either side of the narrow line going to white voters. It was blatant racist corruption, but in North Carolina it's just business as usual.

More volunteers come through the door, all at least twenty years older than you and Tanya. They hug, high-five, and joke. Feeling this unabashed warmth, you know you've done the right thing. Including Tanya and you, there are about a dozen volunteers. Morgan and Clarice step up to the stage. Clarice puts her fingers in her mouth and lets out an ear-piercing whistle. All of you turn your attention to the stage.

"Listen up, y'all. We got a few minutes before the polls open so we gotta get movin' fast."

"We gonna have ourselves a close election," Morgan says. "Even though the state legislature is doing everything in their power to keep us black folks from voting."

"But we gonna show them different, aren't we," Clarice says.

You and the volunteers cheer.

"Here's y'all's assignments," Morgan says as he puts on a pair of glasses hanging around his neck and holds up a clipboard a few inches from his nose. He looks more grandfatherly than bouncer.

The first few names he reads off are for phone calls. When he calls your name with the line "the college boy all the way out here from Chapel Hill,"—which gets oohs and aahs—he says you're going to drive a van to pick up voters.

"I don't know these streets," you tell Tanya after Morgan goes back to the list.

"Yeah, but you'll literally be picking people up." She squeezes your bicep. The touch is electrifying. "They need a strong young man like yourself."

You laugh because you cannot access words. What you wouldn't give to have her touch you again. For decency's sake, you don't allow your mind to venture further.

Morgan makes his way down the stage and slaps his meaty hand on your shoulder. "Come on, son," he says as he guides you to the back door. "I'm gonna show you your set of wheels for the day."

You look back at Tanya, and she gives you little wave and mouths "good luck." Morgan takes you through the gravel parking lot to a beat-up Ford van that has seen better days. You make out the faded words "Pinewood United Baptist Church."

"This is my ride?"

Morgan chuckles, layers of joy jiggling. "That it is. You ain't gonna be pickin' up any hotties in this machine, but you'll be doin' the Lord's work."

You open the door with a loud *screech*. "Hinges could use some oil."

"This machine could use a lot of things. Turn on the radio. See if Tanya's there."

At first you think he's talking about the AM/FM radio, but then you follow Morgan's finger to the CB hanging from the ceiling. You turn on the dial and grab the microphone. You're sure you've seen it done that way in old movies.

"Uh, anybody out there."

"Hey there, Seth," comes Tanya's beautiful voice through the staticky mono speaker. "We hear you loud and clear."

Morgan hands you a clipboard with a page full of names and addresses on it along with blank spots any new voters who may need to be picked up. Next he hands you a map of the town with three locations circled in red.

"These should be the polling stations for most of the voters," Morgan says, pointing his thick finger on the map. "Although there could be more."

You pull up Google Maps on your phone and save the addresses.

Morgan shakes his head. "You don't believe in paper maps, huh?"

"Until you handed me this, I thought they stopped making them."

"Oh, man," Morgan shouts with laughter. "You makin' me feel old."

You smile and turn on the ignition switch. A cloud of blue-gray smoke fills the air.

"See you after everybody votes," you say and put the van in gear.

As you start to roll away, you hear a voice yell, "Wait!" Looking in the side view mirror, Tanya runs up behind the van. Her body in motion is unreal. You brake hard. She makes it to your open window and hands you a thermos of coffee and a bag of donuts.

"A little something to get through the morning," she says with an enchanting smile.

"Thank you. I'll always be happy to take a little something from you."

She grins so big you're not sure if her face can handle it. For that smile you'd wade through a swamp full of alligators without hesitation.

"And I put my number on the bag," she adds. "In case you're away from the CB."

Jackpot. She runs back before you can say anything, so you text her: "ur awesome. thx."

She texts back "good luck" with a brown thumbs-up

emoji.

The first voter is Aida Jones. She lives on 1235 Sycamore Ave. Pulling into the drive, you see an American flag and people waiting in line outside of a church across the street at the end of the corner. That should be easy enough. Maybe you'll walk the old lady over to the polling station and go to the next voter. No need to load her into the van.

Three solid taps later and an old woman with dark skin and contrasting snow-white hair answers the door.

"Hello," she says with a sweet smile.

"I'm here with the Pinewood Community Action Network to take you to your polling station."

"Well good. Ain't no way I can get there myself."

"Just tell me what you'd like me to do. I can walk you over or—"

"Walk me over? Are you out of your mind?"

"Ma'am?"

"My polling station is five miles away. I might look young, but I've put quite a few miles on these hooves and they can't take much more."

"Isn't that your polling station right over there?" You point across the street.

Ms. Jones squints and then digs out a pair of glasses from her purse. "No sir. That's the United Methodist. They in another district."

"But they're right across the street?"

"I know. White folks in Raleigh carved up our community like we were a turkey for Thanksgiving. Here's where I need to go."

She hands you a voter information mailer. On the back is her voting location. 351 N. Davis Street. You consult the map on your phone. It isn't five miles away, but seven.

"Man, that is crazy," you say, leading the lady down to

the van.

"I grew up in a time when we had to take tests to vote. But yes, this is some awful business. People may talk like we equal, but we're far from it."

You open the van's back door and help boost Ms. Jones inside.

Next up is a Gerald Clifford. He is stooped with a cane and dressed in his Sunday best waiting outside his door. He makes his way to the van before you park. After you introduce yourself and open the door for him, you ask where he's supposed to vote.

"At the polling place."

"Do you know which one?"

"The library I reckon."

"You got a photo ID with you like a driver license?"

"Don't drive no more on account of my eyes, but I got my discharge papers from Korea," he says, patting his breast pocket.

You cringe.

"That ain't gonna work," Ms. Jones says from her seat.

He looks up at her. "What you mean it ain't gonna work? I took two bullets in the leg. Bled for my country."

"Any photo ID?" you ask.

Mr. Clifford looks at you, eyes blinking under thick glasses. "What for?"

"How about a birth certificate?"

"Never had one. Was born out in the country."

You rub your forehead knowing this is going to be an issue. But hell, he's a veteran. Even rednecks respect that. Plus you've got more passengers to pick up on a tight timeline.

"Come on Mr. Clifford," you say, helping him into the van. "We'll see what happens."

Six more pickups and the van is full. Everybody should be in district 9, although Tanya says Mr. Clifford's address did not come up in the North Carolina State Board of Elections website. His address seems to on the edge of a narrow curve where the snaking 12th district intersects the 8th and the 9th.

"Weird," she says over the CB. "Why don't you try the library? If he doesn't show up on the registration there, see if he can stay with you and vote at the next station. He's gotta be at one of them."

The first stop is at the library. A statue of Confederate President (or head traitor as you prefer to call him) Jefferson Davis stands across the street in a park. Coming from California, it's been difficult to see all the Confederate nostalgia. Your freaking university has a statue of a confederate solider on campus. People might say it's their heritage, but how could anybody be proud of a history so evil?

You lead your voters to a line that goes out the door. More than one white voter wears clothing with a Confederate flag on it along with a requisite scowl. That you're standing in line with an open hoodie and a black T-shirt underneath with white letters that spell out *BLACK VOTES MATTER* with eight dark-skinned elderly folks seems to invoke discomfort in some folks as they glance over their shoulders and whisper to each other.

Ignore it, you tell yourself. This has happened to you before and not as often as most blacks living in the south. Hell, you even thought as yourself as white (or at least colorless) until second grade when an insecure fourth grader walked up to you in the playground, pointed at your face, and shouted, "Slave." You had no idea what it meant, but you understood his venom and feeling of superiority.

Little racial encounters happened sporadically after that, including the N-word, but for the most part the white people you've met are decent. Your California upbringing helps. Every so often you wonder if you should have accepted that full ride to UNC. Your parents wanted you to stay on the west coast, but you wanted something different. And different is what you found. You'd never seen a real Confederate flag until you moved to the Research Triangle, a place that is about as Californiaesque as you can get when it comes to diversity in the south except for maybe Atlanta.

Regardless, you got "woke" as a freshman, and now you're here to make a difference. Black. American. Citizen.

When your group walks inside, Ms. Jones shows her ID, gets asked a few questions, and then walks over to the electronic voting machine. The next six voters in your group go through the same routine.

"You're next, Mr. Clifford," you say to the veteran, giving him a nudge.

He hobbles up to a white woman behind a folding table.

"Good morning. Who are you?"

"I am Mr. Gerald Clifford from Pinewood. Lived here all my life. Served as gunner in Korea from nineteen fifty to nineteen fifty-two. After that I worked the midnight shift at Reams Furniture Factory for thirty-one years until they went out of business."

The woman takes a ruler and goes through the lists of names.

"I'm sorry, I don't see your name anywhere on our list."

Mr. Clifford's face contorts. "Maybe it's my under my first name, Gerald. Folks get that confused sometimes."

The woman flips pages over and uses the ruler again.

"I'm sorry, not seeing it here either."

You walk up. "Perhaps this isn't your polling place."

The woman scoots back, her eyes wide with fright. "Who are you?"

"I'm here to help Mr. Clifford," you say gently. You're not that imposing of a man. Five-ten and skinny.

"Tryin' to get illegal votes in is what he's tryin' to do," somebody says behind you. "One of those liberal agitators."

You turn to see a man in his sixties, maybe older, with an awful comb-over. He wears an American flag pin on his cardigan because nobody would suspect his nationality if he didn't have one, right? His gray-blue eyes seethe hate through his glasses. A woman, who is probably his wife, puts a hand on his shoulder to quiet him down.

There is so much you want to tell this man starting with where to shove his conspiracy theory, but you take a deep breath instead and turn back to the woman and fake a smile.

"Is it possible to see if he is in this district or any of the other districts polls, ma'am?" "Ma'am" and "sir" are words you've reluctantly taken into your vocabulary out here, but they can work magic in the South.

"I wouldn't be able to do that," she says, her body softening. "I can only see what's on these sheets."

"Does that mean I don't get to vote?" Mr. Clifford asks.

"It means we should try another voting station," you answer, patting him on the back.

You lead Mr. Clifford out the door followed by the glares of a few voters. You're irritated, but don't say anything. Votes are more important than confrontation.

Mr. Clifford stays with you after you drop off the first round of voters and start picking up the next ones. Stopping at an apartment complex you find Maria Garcia dressed in a green sales clerk uniform in apartment 3C. Two beautiful children run around inside, and it looks like a grandmother is taking care of them.

"Thank you so much for the ride. I need to be at the Dollar Store by ten today," she says. "Could you drop me off after I vote?"

"Sure."

Five more pickups, and your van is full with eight passengers including twin sisters and a sulking man in his thirties, Malcolm Edwards. He rides shotgun and tells you he lost his license from a DUI.

"They don't let me drive, but I'm gonna make my vote count. They can't take that from me."

Malcolm turns on the radio. A news station comes on. He switches it over to a hip-hop station. T-Pain. You're down with it.

"Don't y'all play that awful, sinful stuff with me in here," one of the sisters says and suggests a radio channel.

You rotate the old-time knob, and, when you land on the station, it plays gospel music. That gets jeers from the other passengers. Malcolm cracks up. More suggestions are given and debated. You have no idea what to do, so you slowly turn the knob as stations fade in and out. Mr. Clifford likes a country station you come across, but that's an automatic driver's veto.

"How about ninety-six-point-one," Maria says. "It's just generic pop music. Nobody will love it, but nobody should hate it either."

You turn the knob to that approximate station and Ed Sheeran croons. Maria nailed it. It's vanilla. Not your favorite flavor, but okay. Everybody else shrugs, knowing the selections could be worse.

The next polling station is a post office in a different

district three miles away from the library. After parking and helping your group out of the van, all of you join a line that winds out the door. Mr. Clifford tells you stories about Pinewood when he was growing up and how the town was segregated. Malcolm listens in and shakes his head. Some white voters look over at Maria and frown. A few take out their phones and snap photos. Maria stiffens, turning red. You haven't heard anybody say the word *illegal* but you know that's what they're thinking.

A middle-aged white man with a mustache and John Deere hat brings a poll worker to the front door and points at your group. They confer, and then the election man goes back inside. The John Deere enthusiast saunters over. Towering over Maria he says, "I just made sure your illegal vote doesn't count."

"I was born here in America," she says in perfect, unaccented American English. "It is my right to vote as a US citizen."

"Bullshit you were. I know an illegal when I see one."

"Which means anybody with brown skin, doesn't it, asshole?" Maria trembles with rage.

You step in front of her. "Sir, move on please. This lady is a registered North Carolina voter."

"And who do you think you are, boy?"

You swallow, trying to hold your anger inside, but your fists ball hard like boulders, and your body shakes with fear and reddening violence. He takes a step toward you so that you are toe to toe, glaring at each other, neither of you blinking. Through his narrowed eyes you see unfiltered hatred. A crowd gathers. Then a fist swings into your peripheral vision. It lands with a crack on the jackass's jaw. His head jerks back as his green cap flies off. You turn to see Malcolm deliver a follow-up punch to the man's kidney and then take off in a sprint, bursting through the crowd.

You fight the urge to run yourself. Instead you crouch down to help the racist. "You okay, man?"

He massages his jaw. "Who the hell was that?"

"Don't know," you say.

A whoop-whoop siren blares from a police car. It double parks with screeching brakes. You panic, wanting to take off for the hills. Somebody needs to call headquarters and let them know what's going on. You dig out your cell phone and call Tanya.

"Hey there," she says.

"Trouble. Post office. A voter tried to intimidate us."

"Is it still happening?"

"No, he got punched. Police are here."

"On my way."

A police officer runs up, his weapon in hand. You will yourself not to run. Running never works. You've done nothing wrong. Even though your body is shaking, you've gotta take a stand. Be strong for everybody.

"What's happening?" a white officer in his early twenties shouts, his eyes and pistol directed at you.

You point a shaky finger to the man on the ground, your voice unable to speak words. You've never had a gun pointed at you. Is this cop going to kill you? In front of all these people? Several voices answer the officer's question and fingers point in different directions. Most point at you.

"Turn around and put your hands on the wall," the officer shouts at you.

You notice a few cell phones are recording the moment, including, surprisingly, Mr. Clifford.

You find your voice. "What about him? He was the one being aggressive. Trying to intimidate a voter."

Three more cruisers show up. The officers confer, and

you are escorted by a different cop, Officer Reynolds, half a block away to the front of an ice cream shop. Maria is interviewed along with the redneck and a few witnesses. Reynolds is a heavy, pasty white man in his late forties with cruel eyes. He has your driver's license.

"The man came up and started shouting at Ms. Garcia," you tell him. "He was calling her an illegal. It's pure voter intimidation. A federal crime."

"And what is your purpose being here? I see you're from California." He says "California" with derision.

"Scholarship."

"Really?" He looks you over, his eyebrows raised with skepticism.

"Full scholarship to UNC."

"You an athlete?"

"An engineer."

He blinks twice like you told him you're an alien who came to Earth to taste hamburgers. When you reach for your wallet, Reynolds throws his left hand against your chest, shoving you against the wall. His other hand reaches for his pistol.

It happens so fast and unexpectedly your mind is trying to figure out what's happening.

"I-I'm getting my student ID," you say.

"Don't ever make any sudden moves like that," Reynolds says before easing pressure off your chest.

"But you know I'm not packing anything."

"I didn't pat you down. I don't know anything."

Even though the officer provided you an easy slam about his knowledge, you don't go there. Two guns drawn on you in less than five minutes. Insane. Just be happy you're alive.

"Can I show you my ID, sir?"

The officer nods, taking a deep breath. "Yes, but do it

slow."

You reach back slowly and pull out your wallet like you're the subject of a slow motion video shot at 2,000 frames-per-second.

Tanya arrives at the post office by the time your ID is out. She talks to Mr. Clifford who hands her his cell phone.

"You better give me the name of the thug who hit that gentleman over there," Reynolds says, nodding at the John Deere man, "or we'll charge you and you'll never set foot at UNC again."

"Charge me with what?" You know that in the south you're supposed kowtow to authority, but what charges could he bring up? And with Tanya in the distance—who is now talking to an officer with red hair—there ain't no way you're going to look weak.

Reynolds's face flushes. He raises a finger. "Assault for one."

"How? I didn't touch that man. He stepped into my personal space and—"

"Hey, Reynolds," the officer who talked to Tanya calls over. He is standing fifteen feet away with the officer who interviewed John Deere man. He holds up a phone that looks like Mr. Clifford's. "We got video."

"I've seen the sucker punch," Reynolds shouts.

"No. This is before that. It makes things a bit more...hazy."

After Reynolds tells you to stay put, he walks over to the officers. Tanya gives you thumbs up from where she's standing by a police car.

"Hells bells. It's still assault," Reynolds shouts, breaking your trance.

The redhead officer nods your way as he whispers to the other men. Reynolds goes pale as he looks at you and shakes his head in a slow defeated manner.

The redhead officer, McCray according to his name badge, walks over. "This is what we're gonna do. If the man who was assaulted agrees to it, we're gonna drop any charges against you and just forget about this whole incident."

You sense the shift in power and are about to negotiate better terms when Tanya walks over and puts her hand on your shoulder.

"We'll take it," she says.

"But—" you stammer.

"And everybody we brought still gets to vote. Isn't that right, Officer McCray?" she asks.

"Sure thing, Miss Coleman."

You feel a pang of jealousy when the officer smiles at Tanya. She requests to have your group jump to the front of the line, which is good because Maria is already late for her ten AM shift. She is shaken and not too happy, but more determined than ever to vote.

After collecting everybody to the front, you whisper to Tanya, "What did you tell the cops that made them change their tune so quickly?"

"Didn't need to tell them much. Mr. Clifford shot some solid video. Once the man came over, he started recording. I let it speak for itself."

You glance at Mr. Clifford who is looking around the post office, lost in his thoughts. You laugh and shake your head. "Last person I'd expect to know how to use a phone."

"Yeah, old people can surprise sometimes. His video showed that asshole violating federal law." She lowers her voice. "I'm not sure what a Southern white man hates more, a black person with power or federal agents coming down south to enforce laws."

"Number one, I'm pretty sure," you say.

She laughs. "Yeah, but number two isn't far behind."

You lean in close. "For what's its worth, Malcolm got to punch that white asshole for free. I bet that's kind of a once in lifetime opportunity around here."

She nods. "You know it."

Not surprisingly, Mr. Clifford is not on the voter rolls.

"You voted recently, right?" you ask as the three of you walk back outside.

"Voted for Obama."

"Where?" Tanya asks.

"A polling station. I don't remember where. Just went in, told them who I was, and voted. No problem."

"I hope they haven't purged you," you say.

His nostrils flare. "Why would they do that?"

"It's what scared men do," Tanya says.

"I'll take you to the next place, Mr. Clifford," you say. "Hopefully you'll be registered there."

"I hope so," he says.

Maria walks up to you, squeezing her hands together. "Can you take me to work please? My boss is going to be really pissed I'm late."

"It's election day," Tanya says. "You get two hours off."

"You tell that to Jimmy. He's the manager."

Tanya rides with you, taking Malcolm's empty seat, and goes inside the Dollar Store with Maria. From the front window you can see the manager who stands with his arms crossed, shaking his head. He's probably a few years older than you and it looks like he's still battling acne. Whatever Tanya is saying, he's resisting. Folks in the van are commenting about a white boy with too much power in his hands and how they've encountered that before. Finally the manager throws his arms in the air and walks away. Tanya comes out, her eyes are narrowed and lips are tight in a hard frown. She gets in and slams the door.

"What an asshole."

"Language!" a twin says.

"Sorry about that."

"Everything worked out?" you ask.

"I don't know. He wants to fire her mighty bad. Had planned to do it today because she was late, but I convinced him his ass...butt would be on the line if he did it. I also asked him if he was giving his other employees time off to vote. He isn't too happy. I'll make sure Morgan looks after Maria."

You drive Tanya back to her car and then drop everybody else off. You pick up more voters, and then you drive to the third district of the morning. The church building down the street from Ms. Jones' house. The voters in line are mixed race. You're surprised when Mr. Clifford is on the registration file.

"Hallelujah!" he says. "This is the third place we've tried."

"I'm glad you finally found us," a black woman says from behind a table. "We just need your ID." Her kind smile turns to a frown when Mr. Clifford pulls out his Army discharge papers and hands it to her. "Oh. This is gonna be tough."

"Hasn't been before," Mr. Clifford says. "People used to respect the service."

A bearded white man walks over with a grimace on his face. "I'm sorry, but if you don't have any of the following IDs you can't vote."

He hands Mr. Clifford a pamphlet. It has a list of approved IDs including driver's license, passports, etc, all of which have to be up to date and have a photo. You know what it asks for and the racist reasons behind the law.

"What are you sayin' is that although I got me a Purple Heart and a Bronze Star," he pulls two medals from his jacket, "I can't vote?"

"I'm sorry, but it ain't gonna do," the man says, crossing his arms. "I'm following the law."

"Wanna see my goddamn scars?"

Before you know what is happening, Mr. Clifford has loosened his belt and dropped his pants on the floor.

"Whoa there," you say, reaching for the pants puddled around his ankles.

People in line guffaw and laugh.

"Here and here," Mr. Clifford says pointing to shiny round scars on his thigh and his calf. "You see that? Got 'em both at Heartbreak Ridge. You see what I've done to earn my right to vote."

The man flushes.

"Come on, man, give him a provisional ballot," you say, helping Mr. Clifford pull his pants back up.

"Do you at least got an electric bill?" he asks.

"My nephew pays it."

"Let him vote," somebody shouts in the line. Then another person shouts it. Suddenly people, black and white, are chanting "let him vote." Even other poll workers are chanting. Goosebumps rise on your arms. Mr. Clifford holds his head up, chin high. Cell phones are out, recording this amazing moment. This is how unity works. People coming together to help each other.

The poll worker's face turns tomato red. "Fine. I'll let you do a provisional ballot."

"Give me a paper ballot or a wooden one," Mr. Clifford says. "I don't care. Just let me vote."

The man hands him a ballot. "But we're gonna make

sure you are who you say you are."

People in line cheer when Mr. Clifford takes the ballot and hobbles over to a booth. When he comes back, you help him fill out the information on the sheet, put in an envelope, and hand it over to the man.

"Happy now?" the poll worker says to you.

"Give me the tracking number on the ballot so we can make sure it goes through."

The man grumbles, writes down a series of numbers, and hands you the paper. Folks in line congratulate Mr. Clifford, patting him on the arm and thanking him for his service.

After you drop everybody back at their homes, it's past noon. Tanya tells you to drive back to P-CAN so you can have some pizza. You hightail it over there, knowing you wouldn't drive any slower if she had offered you boiled cabbage.

Sitting next to Tanya, you munch through three combo slices, swig a glass of Coke, and give a quick rundown about Mr. Clifford dropping trou. Morgan cannot stop laughing, and it is contagious. Your sinuses burn after Coke comes up your nose, which causes everybody to laugh harder.

Before you know it, you're back on the road picking up a new round of voters. There are more speed bumps with people at the wrong polls because of the gerrymandering, which make things difficult for people who wanted to vote for specific candidates in mind. But it's becoming routine now.

Four more pick ups, votes, and drop offs, and it is after seven PM.

"Great job, Seth," Tanya says. "Head on back to headquarters."

Her words sound like Peter opening the pearly gates after a life devoted to good works.

You walk inside the center at seven-fifteen. Kool and the Gang's *Celebration* blasts through the speakers. Morgan pulls some dope moves as he bounces around, a huge smile on his face. Clarice and a few other ladies join him, looking silly and having the time of their lives.

"Come on, son," Morgan says, waving you over.

You smile and shake your head.

"Don't wanna make an ass out of yourself?" Tanya says, walking over.

"I've done that enough already today."

The two of you talk over the dance tunes from the last century like Michael Jackson and Paula Abdul. You are mere inches away from Tanya and desperately want to kiss her. Maybe ask her to dance first? You can't find the words. You feel like you're thirteen again at an awkward school dance. You resolve to ask her after Whitney's "I Wanna Dance With Somebody," but the music cuts off mid-chorus.

"They're startin' to do the counts," Clarice shouts.

All of you crowd around a forty-inch screen as Charlotte newscasters talk about voting projections for the entire state. Republicans seem to have the lead in most of the rural areas as expected. Democrats have parts of Raleigh, Charlotte, and the minority-majority 12th district that runs throughout the state.

"Just projections," Morgan says with confidence. "Projections based on one or two percent of the ballots being counted."

BBQ is ordered as you keep your eye on the three districts where you drove around. One is not going to go your way. The minority-majority is as expected. And then there's that third district, where Mr. Clifford finally voted. It's a toss up for the state representatives, and the Republican incumbent for US Congress is squeaking by with fifty-one percent. There are hoots, cheers, and high-fives, although it is too early to tell. At some point you put your arm around Tanya and she leans into you. Your heart thuds rapidly. This might be the best day of your life.

When the BBQ comes you don't want take your arm away in spite of how wonderful the pulled pork smells.

"Wanna eat?" she asks.

"Yeah, but I kind of like it here with you."

"Me too," she whispers in your ear. You think you might burst when she slaps your thigh. "But if I don't eat soon I'll get cranky, and I don't want to be that way around you."

Both of you walk over to a spread of smoked meat, buns, and sauce. Your mouth waters like a cartoon wolf. This is a just reward for hard day's work.

By ten o'clock enough ballots have been counted for candidates to either concede or celebrate. Republicans are still going to control the state, but two of your districts swung Democrat. The Republican Congressman on the ropes will go back to DC, but barely. Depending on how the final tally comes out, there might be a recount.

You know all of this not from the television, but from your car radio where you've been making out with Tanya in the backseat.

"We're gonna have a hard time explaining ourselves if we stay any later," she says.

When you walk back in holding Tanya's hand, the ladies give you devilish smiles and Morgan shoots questioning, sideways glower, but man, you feel like you're the king of the universe. With Tanya by your side nobody, not even a racist president, can stop you from your dreams.

The party breaks up around 10:30, and Tanya walks you to your car. She wants you to stay.

"Look, I'm not leavin' 'til tomorrow. You can stay at Uncle Morgan's tonight."

"He ain't going to let me get close to you under his roof."

"True enough. He'll make you sleep on the couch, but after he's asleep,"—her eyebrows lift—"you know what I'm sayin'?"

You know what she's saying and you would love more than anything in the world to spend more time with Tanya, but you need to be at Dr. Steiner's Advanced Structural Engineering at eight in the morning, and you've got a two and half hour drive ahead. The professor's not known to excuse absences, even legit Granny's-in-the-hospital ones.

You kiss Tanya, long and hard as she rubs her hands on your back and squeezes below that. Maybe you will stay the night. She ends the kiss and pushes you away. "Go home, engineer. But you text me when you get there. I wanna make sure you make it safe."

"You know I will. And maybe I'll call you tomorrow night and the night after that."

"You better. Until we meet again?"

"Until we meet again."

She smiles, and it's like a tractor beam. You swoop in for another kiss. It's quick, but powerful.

"Bye, Tanya."

"See you, Seth. And watch out for speed traps with redneck cops."

You laugh as you open the door. Starting up the engine, you give a final wave and drive away.

You question your sanity for the second time today, wondering how you could leave Tanya. Yes, your scholarship depends on maintaining a high GPA, but dammit, she's worth academic probation. You will more than call her this weekend. You'll drive over to Wake Forest and see her in the flesh.

Rolling down the window, you feel a cold draft of air explode into the car. The chill sweeps away the fatigue, making you feel alive. You turn up the radio, Jay Z pumping loud. In that moment life is wonderful. Your future is laid out in front of you. You'll get a PhD in structural engineering, and Tanya will get her law degree. Together you'll change the world for the better. You'll build bridges and roads that will be cost effective and last forever while she'll bridge communities and fight for equality. Your children will do even more than that. People can make a difference. Look what both of you did today. She coordinated and you transported more than fifty voters to the polls who otherwise would not be able to do so. Wonderful and uplifting thoughts about the present and future swirl through your head before flashing red and blue lights disrupt the darkness about a mile away from the highway entrance.

It will come out later that this particular part of the road is an infamous speed trap where a posted, but foliage-hidden speed limit sign drops from 45 to 35 MPH. Mark Corrigan, the cop who pulls you over, has a history of violence and is going through his second divorce. But you don't know this. You keep your hands on the wheel, ten and two. Heart thumping loudly. Radio off. You watch the silhouetted officer grow larger in the side view mirror as he approaches. His left hand holds a flashlight, his right is on his weapon. You flinch as the blinding light strikes your eyes.

"License and registration," he says.

"What did I do, officer?"

"Speeding in a posted thirty-five mile an hour zone. License and registration."

"I didn't see any sign. I was looking."

"License and registration," he orders just under a shout.

You swallow and grip the steering wheel to keep your hands from shaking. You are pissed. This is not the way you want to finish the night. No doubt the cop is an insecure asshole, getting off on the power of a tin badge. You want to call him out and confront his assumed authority. Especially after today. But fear tweaks your system. How many brothers have been killed in similar circumstances? You don't want to be a statistic.

"May I reach for my wallet?" you ask and then add the requisite, "Sir?" Saying the last word burns your soul.

"Yes, but slow."

Feeling déjà vu, you pull out your wallet and then the driver's license in slow motion. You feel palpable anger when the cop sees your California ID. What is the deal with all of the hatred against your home state? It's like jealousy on steroids.

"Registration," he demands.

"It's in the glove box."

"Well get it then."

A beam of light tracks your hand as you reach over. You pull on the latch, but it is locked. Dammit. There has been a wave of campus parking lot burglaries. Upset at forgetting and aching with humiliation, you swing your arm up to grab the keys in the ignition.

The officer yells "Stop!" and then your body jerks involuntarily as gunshots explode. Four bullets slam into your upper torso.

You don't feel pain. Too much adrenaline and confusion for that. And you're fading. Sadness looms over you. You know you won't get a PhD. Won't see your parents or sister. And you'll never kiss Tanya again. As your consciousness drifts, your mind accesses a final memory: that last kiss. Tanya's wide smile and bright hopeful eyes. Your head slumps forward as you relive that moment when the world was perfect.

About Travis Richardson

Travis Richardson was born in Germany, raised in Oklahoma and has spent recent years in northern and southern California. He enjoys writing. When he's not working at UCLA, he keeps busy writing, reading, watching movies or shooting them. He edited *Ransom Notes*, the Los Angeles Sisters in Crime monthly newsletter for several years.

He also reviewed Anton Chekhov's short stories at Chekhovshorts.com and pens a monthly blog post at Writing Wranglers and Warriors.

Travis is widely published as a short story writer, with works in *The Obama Inheritance*, *Jewish Noir*, *Locked and Loaded* and many other magazines and anthologies. His short story "Final Testimony" is a finalist for a 2018 Derringer award.

To learn more about Travis Richardson, visit http://www.tsrichardson.com/.

WHO IS STUART BRIDGE?

JAMES W. ZISKIN

TAMMY:

I WAS AT THE beauty parlor, just about to go under the dryer, when Cousin Janey phoned. She said it was urgent. Well, I couldn't very well rush over to the nursing home with a wet head, could I? Appointments are hard to get at La Belle Mademoiselle. And my hair had to look nice for Daddy's re-election campaign the next day. You know my father is a United States congressman, don't you? Of course you do. Everybody knows that. So I lied and told Janey I was on my way. A little white lie. There was the little matter of a facial first. And since I was already sitting in the chair, the girl did my nails, too. Carelessly, I might add. She made a mess of the whole thing, and the polish didn't dry properly. She tried to say I was rushing her. I adjusted her tip accordingly and gave her a piece of my mind, too. It's only right. A gratuity is for good service, after all.

Anyhow, as soon I could, I rushed over to be with Janey and Uncle Henry at the home. She told me he'd tried to say something but she couldn't quite understand what. I was tempted to tell her that hardly amounted to "urgent" in my book. But I'm a kind soul and took her fragile state into account and kept my thoughts to myself. She was all alone in the world except for her daddy—poor thing—and he didn't have much time left on the meter, as we now know all too well. I asked her to take a couple of breaths and start from the beginning

She began to sob and gulp for air in her usual fashion, like a fish flopping around on the ground. It's not nice to laugh at her, of course, but the spectacle *is* quite comical. Sorry about that. What I meant to say is that's what she's always done when she gets emotional. Gasp like a fish. Then she usually gets the hiccups. Still does to this day, even at forty-nine. Same age as me, though people tell me I look younger. Do I look younger to you? Sorry. Never mind.

Now where was I? Oh, yes. So Janey finally calmed down, and I pressed her to tell me exactly what her daddy had done. She repeated that he'd sat up in the bed and mumbled something she couldn't make out. And then the waterworks started again. I gave her a big hug and comforted her, all the while trying to keep her slobbering off my new hairdo. She's my best friend in the world, but I'd just had it styled the way I like it. You understand, don't you? Of course you do. Well, besides being my cousin— more like my sister, really—Janey's my best friend in the world. Always has been. We don't neither one of us have any brothers or sisters, you see, and ever since we were little girls, we've been inseparable.

So with the big drama of her daddy sitting up in bed forgotten, we settled in and visited for a while. She told me my hair looked nice, and I felt bad for lying to her earlier. Uncle Henry was out of it like he'd been for the past several weeks. Just staring at the ceiling tiles, unshaven and dribbling out of the side of his mouth onto the pillow. Non-responsive, the doctors called him. Trapped inside his own head. Or maybe he was looking up at Aunt April in heaven, talking sweet nothings to her like he used to do. What a wonderful couple they made. Fifty-one years of wedded bliss. Old-fashioned love, the way it used to be. *Good* love. Not like the sick lust you see today, what with folks doing as they please when they please and with whom they please. Well, what can you do?

Anyway, Poor Uncle Henry had been going downhill for, oh, probably the last year and a half. Always in decline. Bedsores, senile ramblings, soiling himself...We've all got that to look forward to, I don't have to tell you. But he had some good moments, too, every so often. One day he'd forget your name—even Janey's—then he was okay for another short while. But just a little worse each time. Such a cruel thing to watch, dementia. Of course it's bad for the patient, too.

Can I confess something to you? You know, despite my love for Uncle Henry, I was hoping for an end to his suffering. The doctors said a recovery was out of the question, so, yes, I'm almost ashamed to say I wished he'd just go ahead and get it over with already. Go to his eternal reward, you know? Die. And now that he's gone, I suppose it's a mercy for Janey, too. Poor thing.

And yet just two years ago, before Aunt April passed

away, he was still working full time at the firm he and my daddy built. If there was an ambulance to be chased or a corporation to be sued, Uncle Henry was on it faster than a New York Jewish lawyer. I mean that as a compliment, by the way. The love of money is to their credit. I've got nothing against the Jewish people. But back to Uncle Henry. You couldn't tear him away from the office unless it was for a court date, a tee time, or drinks at the club. Or, of course, Fox News. Oh, my, how he loved Fox News. Almost as much as he loved Aunt April, rest her soul. But I'll let you in on a little secret: he hated Obama! You probably saw that coming, didn't you? Hated all Democrats, really, which was curious since he'd been one himself until 1965. A Dixiecrat, actually. Not quite the same thing anymore, I guess. I remember he used to thank Jesus for striking down his own daddy—my granddaddy—before he ever had to accept the "apocalyptic truth," turn coat, and register *Republican*. And don't get me started on what he thought of Communists, foreigners, and integrationists.

Yes, it's a shame he's gone. You know, Uncle Henry was a very handsome man. Not tall, but well built with a strong jaw, fine white teeth, and the prettiest blue eyes you ever saw. Oh, yes. And he had charisma to burn. The ladies at the country club sure liked him. Aunt April had to suffer his flirty ways, because he definitely enjoyed chatting with the girls. I can only imagine how many hearts he broke when he was a young man. Played end on the football team and ran anchor in the 400-yard relay. Big man on campus at college.

Yes, he was handsome. Now Poor Janey, on the other hand, was never blessed in the looks department. The boys didn't exactly beat a path to her door, if you catch my drift. Strange, though. You'd think she'd have turned out more comely than she did, given how good-looking Uncle Henry was. But sometimes a girl favors her father a little too much physically, and the result is horsey. That's Janey to a T. Also ran. Like a horse.

Not that I'm any prize this side of a 4-H tent. You wouldn't know it to look at me today, but in my younger days I was plenty popular with the boys. I might've greased the skids a bit on that score. In high school I was known as a good sport, if you know what I mean.

Just listen to me. Talking about age and looks after such a tragedy. A lady shouldn't do that, should she? Where was I? Oh, yes. Uncle Henry was flat on his back, and Janey and I were discussing this and that. And then he stirred in his bed. He hadn't moved a muscle in weeks, if you didn't count his bowels. Oh, and of course the one time earlier that day when Janey interrupted my hair appointment. We went to check on him, and what should happen but the man who hadn't uttered a coherent word in weeks suddenly sat up and hollered as clear as a bell that he was sorry for what he'd done.

We nearly jumped out of our skins. It was eerie. His voice was rough. Otherworldly, I'd describe it as. Desperate but pleading at the same time. He froze there in the bed, eyes clenched shut, and Janey and I wondered for a moment if we might've imagined it all.

"Do you think we might've imagined it all?" I asked her.

But before she could answer he spoke again.

"I am truly sorry, Lord!" he bellowed. "Sorry for what I did. Forgive this sinner!" and more such nonsense.

Janey asked him what he was sorry for, and he answered in a softer voice, "For the terrible thing…" Wait…Give me a moment. This is difficult for me to repeat because it's just so wrong what he said about my daddy. It simply can't be.

He said...Uncle Henry said he and his brother, Lee—that's my daddy—had done a terrible thing many years ago.

"Stuart Bridge," he said, almost in a whisper.

That didn't make any sense to Janey, and not to me either. Surely this was a nightmare of some kind.

"Who is Stuart Bridge?" she asked all gentle like.

The question sent him into a rage. He shook and thrashed in the bed, screaming to high heaven and failing his arms, kicking his feet, and speaking in tongues. At least that's what it sounded like to me. Uncle Henry didn't seem to know us or even realize we were there. His face grew redder with each roar, his eyes too, until we thought he was going to have a stroke and drop dead right then and there.

But he went quiet instead. His body slackened like a piece of rope, and he fell back onto his pillow just as a nurse arrived at a run, looking like she expected to find us strangling the patient with the sash of his own bathrobe or something. Of course she wanted to know what in the hell was going on. But before Janey and I even had a chance to shrug, Uncle Henry spoke again, this time firm and clear.

He said Stuart Bridge wasn't a man. It was a place. The place where him and my daddy used to go when they were boys to catch frogs and smoke the cigarettes they stole.

"A wooden bridge," he said. "At Leffert's Creek. It's gone now. But that's where we did it."

"Did what, Daddy?" Janey asked him.

He drew a breath, and I thought it might be his last. Kind of wish it had been now, given the awful thing he said next. But he kept on breathing.

"The boys from Baltimore," he said, his eyes open and focused somewhere on the ceiling. "The ones who died in the car crash. Fifty years ago."

"Fifty years ago?" asked Janey, close to blubbering again.

I just knew she'd be making her fish-face before too long. "Boys from Baltimore?"

"The meddling liberals who came down to register black folks to vote," he announced, almost like he was impatient to have to do so. "They came down from Baltimore to interfere in things that weren't none of their concern."

Janey turned to me, but I was as confused as she was.

He spoke fast and normal now, like he wasn't senile with age—which he was—and everything he was saying wasn't lies and crazy nightmares—which it was, too. None of it true. But I'll tell it to you as he said it, even if it pains me to repeat such calumnies against my own daddy. Of all people! My daddy is the sweetest man in the world. A loving and kind father. And a fine husband to my mama. A respected lawyer and a God-fearing lay minister, if you please. And if that isn't enough, well, as you know, he's a United States congressman!

I'm sorry. Just give me a moment to compose myself.

All right. I think I can continue now. As I was saying, Uncle Henry claimed the two of them—him and my daddy—chased those two boys out of Colored Town, to Route 57, and onto Garland Road. He paused to lick his dry lips. Then...oh, my, this is difficult. Then he said they rammed 'em. Tried to scare 'em. Run 'em off the road. And those boys from Baltimore lost control of their car on Stuart Bridge and flipped into Leffert's Creek. They drowned in eight feet of water.

His exact words were, "Me and Lee killed them. We did, Lord. We killed those boys, and I regret what we did." And...Then...And then he died.

Forgive me. I'm still emotional about it. Thankfully I have a dignified way of crying. Unlike Janey, poor dear.

And of course none of what he said is true. Uncle Henry

was a fine man. Even if he was against integration back then—who wasn't?—he didn't have a racist bone in his body and never would've hurt another soul. And that goes double for my daddy. No, it was as if Uncle Henry fell off his rocker and bumped his head to say such a crazy thing. Senile old folks are prone to the most embarrassing outbursts, after all. He got himself confused and twisted into a knot, thinking he'd done some poor soul wrong once upon a time. That was how good he was. But no matter what he said in his delirious state, fancy or plain, sincere and contrite, it was a bad dream. And none of that changes a thing either way. My daddy never killed nobody.

So that's the story. The truth. The insult to injury, of course, is that nosy nurse. She was right there to hear it all. And she took advantage of the situation and went to the police to spread the deranged ravings of a senile man. Whatever will happen to Daddy's reputation if this gets out? Those Democrats are sure to make a fuss and demand his resignation. That's all they ever do is complain and call for resignations. But what about the people of this district who voted for Daddy? I ask you. What about those fine folks? Would the liberals deny them their voice? It's downright unAmerican, I say. Oh, I can't bear to think about it.

CHIEF PUCKETT:

Now don't you fret, Tammy. I knew your Uncle Henry, and I know your daddy, too. By the way, please do convey my regards to the honorable congressman, will you? And I don't think we need to give this ugly incident another thought. Your poor uncle is at peace now. A gentleman, he was, who loved his fellow man so that in his final moments, in his sickened state, he confused a long-forgotten accident for something it wasn't.

And it wouldn't be right to smear your daddy's reputable name. Did I ask you to convey my regards to him? I did? Well, please do.

Thank you for coming in to make your statement. Consider the case closed.

About James W. Ziskin

James Ziskin is the author of the Anthony® and Macavity Award-winning Ellie Stone Mysteries. His books have also been finalists for the Edgar®, Barry, and Lefty awards. A linguist by training, he studied Romance Languages and Literature at the University of Pennsylvania. After completing his graduate degree, he worked in New York as a photo-news producer and writer, and then as Director of NYU's Casa Italiana. He spent fifteen years in the Hollywood post production industry, running large international operations in the subtitling/ localization and visual effects fields. His international experience includes two years working and studying in France, extensive time in Italy, and more than three years in India. He speaks Italian and French.

James grew up in Amsterdam, New York. He now lives in Seattle.

To learn more about James, visit https:// jameswziskin.com.

Bombs Away

Mariah Klein

Olivia watched in horror as three police cars screeched to a halt in front of the church. Sirens wailed. Red and blue lights flashed like fireworks. She'd expected something to go wrong today. Had spent months preparing for every eventuality. It was still a shock when the worst happened.

Olivia raced over to one of the cars, her boots clunking on the hard ground. A wiry white man in uniform, eyes shaded by mirrored sunglasses, slammed his car door. He held up a rigid hand in front of her face. Olivia skidded to a stop, careful not to make physical contact. She saw herself as a nineteen-year-old college student and community organizer. He would see her as one thing only: angry black woman.

"What's the problem?" Olivia asked. "What's

happening? Sir?"

The last word made her choke, but here in the heartland, formalities were required. Ferguson was not far away, in miles or memory. She tried to manage a smile despite her heart pounding beneath her university sweatshirt.

"Bomb threat," the officer growled. "We're evacuating."

"Bomb threat?" Olivia repeated. "This is a polling place."

"It's closed now, lady." He raised his voice and pointed behind her. "Go to the road and stay there."

A swarm of police surged out of cars and into the building. Olivia glanced over her left shoulder. Far in the distance, she could make out a vehicle churning prairie dust into the overcast midday sky. That would be Peter, driving a school bus full of rural folks they'd arranged to bring on their lunch breaks. Poor people who had neither the time nor the means to drive themselves an hour just to vote. People whose voices mattered. And she'd gotten them here. Just in time for a bomb threat.

Selena and Will ran out of the church. Selena's dreadlocks bounced on her shoulders and tumbled over her yellow sweatshirt with the words *Black Lives Matter* in bold across the front. Will's white face looked pasty, his collared shirt loosened at the top. He pushed his glasses up on his nose. Her soldiers in the fight against voter suppression. Both stared at her in dismay, waiting for instructions.

"He said there's a bomb." Selena jerked a thumb over her shoulder. "They're getting everyone out. Closed indefinitely."

Olivia watched the policemen escort Ms. Phyllis and Ms. Rose out of the church. The civil rights veterans seemed old and frail next to the men. The poll workers had been Olivia's inspiration. They'd marched with Dr. King and boycotted grapes with César Chávez. Now they were being led out of a church by policemen. Rage simmered in Olivia's heart. Votes denied. Again.

"Selena," she barked. "Go meet Peter. Don't let him leave. People will vote here, and they'll vote today. I promise."

Selena nodded and ran down the road. Will coughed next to Olivia. She ignored him. She'd spotted the sheriff, looking self-important in his wide-brimmed hat. Olivia trotted toward him, smoothing her hair into its tight bun. She might be trembling inside, but her outside would look professional and calm. Even if it killed her.

"Excuse me, sir," Olivia said in her most respectful voice. "We have a group of voters on their way, and I'd like to know what to tell them."

"Tell them to go home." The sheriff tipped his hat back to look at her. "We got a call there's a bomb in this church. We have to check it out."

"How long will that take?" She added a smile to soften the question.

"As long as it has to." The sheriff smiled too, but it didn't soften his words. "Your voters best find somewhere else."

"There's nowhere else." Olivia's voice tightened. "The next polling place is twenty miles away."

"Too bad." The sheriff frowned. "No one enters this parking lot until we've cleared the scene. No vote's worth someone's life."

Olivia watched him stride away. She didn't want anyone to get hurt today. But for all she knew, there was no bomb threat. It was an excuse to close down a poll and disenfranchise black people. She had to admit the strategy was clever. Who would ever know?

"What do we do now?" Will appeared at her side.

Olivia looked at Will's pale face and messy black hair. His geekiness had been attractive once. Now she wished he'd show a little more gumption. She'd have to solve this problem herself.

"I'm going in," she said.

Olivia ran around the outside of the church, crouching low to avoid the attention of the officers supposedly securing the scene. She suspected their true intention was to close the place long enough for the black folks to go home without voting. Maybe the votes already cast today would get "lost." Olivia vowed to herself that would not happen. She needed to get inside and see what the police were doing. Maybe even record them on her cell phone.

She reached for the door to the storm cellar under the church. The sound of her name made her jump. Olivia whirled around. Will stood there, twitching with anxiety.

"You can't go in there." Will wrung his hands. "What if there's a bomb?"

"Listen to me." Olivia put her hands on Will's shoulders. "There is no bomb. You've been working with us for months. You know we expected something like this."

"I know, but—" Will bit his lip. "What if it's not a trick?"

"It's a trick." Olivia heaved an exasperated sigh. "But think what you want. I'm going in."

Olivia clattered down the stairs to the cellar. She could hear Will follow her into the gloom. Maybe he wasn't a frightened rabbit after all. Or maybe he liked her enough to conquer his fear. Olivia slowed her steps while her eyes adjusted to the darkness. She didn't slow quickly enough. Her foot hit something hard. A stack of hymnals tipped over, falling to the floor with a crash. She cringed and stayed put while the dust settled.

"Olivia," Will hissed. "I don't like this. Let's go back."

"Hush." Olivia held up a hand.

Something wasn't right. She held her breath. If only Will would do the same. His shallow breathing was all she could hear. She spun in a slow circle, every sense on high alert.

Olivia's eyes fell on a dark pile of fabric. A faint red light blinked beneath the cloth. She walked with measured steps to the lump. Then knelt down in front of it. Behind her, Will whimpered. Olivia lifted the edge of the fabric. She sucked in a breath.

Six sticks of explosives tied together. A box with a blinking red light. The only thing missing was a digital clock counting down the seconds. Dread bloomed in Olivia's stomach. She slowly let the fabric down over the device and turned with wide eyes to look at Will.

He had his phone out in his hands. His fingers jabbed frantically at the screen. Will's eyes behind his glasses seemed huge. In the electronic light, Olivia could see a sheen of sweat on his upper lip.

"No service," he whispered.

"Run," Olivia commanded.

They beat it to the stairs, Olivia treading on Will's heels. They burst out of the storm cellar and ran for the field behind the church. Olivia's mind raced as fast as her feet. There had actually been a bomb. Thank God, the old ladies had been evacuated. She thought of the people who had voted this morning. They had stood directly over a ticking bomb while exercising their inalienable right to vote. The thought made her ill. Olivia closed her eyes just for a second.

That was a mistake. Will had slowed down in front of her, and she barreled into him. They fell in a heap onto the hard prairie ground. Will's phone flew out of his hand. Olivia scrambled up and retrieved it. They had to alert the sheriff. And Selena and Peter, to tell them to keep everyone away. Olivia looked down at the phone in her hand and froze.

The screen of Will's phone blinked with an urgent red light. *Deactivation initiated*, she read. *Enter code.* Below were six lines. A six-digit code would deactivate the bomb under the church. She slowly turned her head and stared at Will. Her mind, ever paranoid, had not anticipated this.

He lay sprawled on the ground, looking up at her with fear in his eyes. She took a step toward him. She wanted to throttle the man. And then kick herself hard in the behind for ever trusting him. Will's eyes strayed to his watch. She stopped short. First things first.

"Give me the code, Will." Her voice was laced with steel. "Before you kill someone."

"I'll shut it off," he said. "Just promise you won't turn me in."

"Are you crazy?" Olivia shrieked. Part of her knew she should promise anything just to get him to turn the thing off. But some things were impossible.

"I was going to turn it off." Will raised his voice. "It was just for a scare. Give it to me, Olivia. Time's running out."

From the crack in his voice, she believed him about the time. But she wasn't about to give him his phone back. For all she knew, he'd run off and the bomb would explode anyway. The only chance she had was keeping the device in her hands.

"Why, Will?" She took one step back, holding the phone over her head. "Why would you do this?"

"Oh, Jesus." Will ran a trembling hand through his hair. "I had to. I didn't know anyone when I moved here. These guys befriended me. They had this idea and I couldn't say no."

Olivia knew who he meant. The KKK was alive and well in these parts. She just hadn't pegged Will for what he was. She'd have a hard time forgiving herself for that.

"I don't want to hurt anyone," Will pleaded. "And I don't want to go to jail. Please, Olivia. Give me the phone."

"Tell me the code," she yelled.

Will looked again at his watch. His eyes flew back to hers. He got to his feet and came toward her. She clutched the phone to her chest.

"Less than a minute, Olivia." His voice cracked with desperation. "I don't want it to go off. I swear."

"Why should I believe you?" she asked.

"I'm not like them." Another step closer. Then another. "Once I got to know you, I didn't want to go through with it. After you kissed me—"

Olivia clocked him. She couldn't help herself. He'd had to bring up that kiss they'd shared, to throw it in her face that she'd kissed a racist. Even had feelings for him for a hot minute. She shook out her stinging knuckles. His body crumpled at her feet. Ten years of Muay Thai boxing meant she knew how to place a punch.

Olivia stared at the phone in her hands. She had seconds to break a six-digit code. One chance to get it right. Olivia looked down at the huddled figure. She'd taken him out, and she could stop this bomb too. She had to. Olivia took a breath, said a prayer, and typed in six numbers.

Hours later, the police and the defunct bomb were gone. The sheriff had handcuffed Will personally. He hadn't exactly thanked Olivia, but he'd allowed the poll to re-open.

Olivia stood next to Selena and watched with pride as the line of twenty rural voters filed through the voting booth. Ms. Phyllis and Ms. Rose congratulated each person as they affixed an "I Voted" sticker to every lapel. Selena turned to Olivia.

"I can't believe you deactivated a bomb," she said. "Doesn't get more bad-ass than that."

"I couldn't have done it," Olivia said. "If the dirtbag hadn't used my birthday as the code."

She looked at Selena. Selena looked at her. And the two women began to laugh.

About Mariah Klein

Mariah Klein is a mystery reader and writer in the San Francisco Bay Area. A former elementary school teacher, she now works for a university, translating the state teacher credentialing requirements into something you actually want to read. She lives with her husband, two daughters and a son, and secretly aspires to be Jessica Fletcher, who somehow managed to be a best-selling mystery writer while traversing the world and solving mysteries. This short story is her first published work. You can read her blog at www.mariahklein.com and follow her on Twitter @MariahJKlein.

Bombs Away won the Short Story, Mystery/Thriller, Adult prize in the San Mateo County Fair's Literary Contest 2018.

TWELVE, ANGRY

CATRIONA MCPHERSON

IN MY HEAD, IN MY mind's eye kind of thing, in my dreams it turned out, today was a win. Today was triumph and satisfaction. Today was initiative and enterprise and freedom. It was a celebration. It was poetic justice. It was *meant to be*.

I'd wheedled and whined at my mum and got nowhere but when I wheeled out the symbolism of it she threw up her hands in surrender and let them fall back down against her thighs with the soft clap of defeat.

I packed carefully. A notebook, two pens, a cardi even though it was boiling hot, a brolly even though the sky was depthless blue from horizon to horizon and had been for weeks now. I took my Walkman with my Joy Division tape in case anyone was watching and *Off The Wall* for real. I had my train fare, some extra for a Coke, and a tenner in my shoe for emergencies.

The station was easy. There's only two platforms. The trains go one way to Edinburgh and the other way to Glasgow with a footbridge over the lines between them.

'Just you?' an old man said to me, behind me in the ticket queue. He wasn't a stranger, I'd seen him chatting to my dad over the front-garden wall off and on my whole life.

'Just me,' I said. 'I'm going to the central library.'

'Homework, is it?'

'History project,' I said. 'Suffragettes.'

'Suffragettes!' All the wrinkles disappeared from round his eyes as he opened them wide. 'You're young for that, aren't you? And you're young to be getting the train on your lonesome.'

'I'm nearly thirteen,' I told him. Then I was at the ticket window and had to turn away. I wished he hadn't said "lonesome". Or I wished he'd got into the same compartment as me. But he headed for smoking and I'd promised my mum not to.

When I was wee, like tiny, I had a harness and reins made of pink leather with soft white fur on the wrong side. The breastplate had a flaking painting of two rabbits on it. There was a mummy rabbit with a shopping basket and Minnie Mouse shoes and a baby rabbit with a bow on her head and an ice-lolly in her hand. It always bothered me. I got the message: wear your reins like a good girl and you can go shopping with Mummy. If you're lucky you might get ice-cream too. But the rabbit in the picture wasn't wearing reins so I added them with a red felt-tip and got shouted at for spoiling something pretty,

Later, I was trusted to walk on my own, on the inside of the pavement away from the cars, only holding her hand at the crossing. Later still, I crossed the roads solo. She'd watch from the gate till I was safely over and in the winter if choir ran late and it was dark my dad would come and collect me, waiting in the warm car with the news on the radio, his clothes smelling like whatever my mum was cooking.

After this summer, this endless scorching summer, I'd be getting a bus to school and back. I'd be miles away all day, even over lunchtime. I told them that, campaigning for today. I'd been in town loads of times, I reminded them. Too old for reins and hand holding, I'd traipsed the length of Princes Street in search of school shoes or a winter coat.

Stepping down onto the platform at Waverley this afternoon, though, it seemed different. I hadn't known, all those other times, on all those shopping trips, that my mum was leading the way, that I was following her.

Now I remembered how she'd touch me. She'd lay her fingers gently against my arm, saying "this way, this way" without words. Today, alone, I stood in the middle of the concourse, strangers rushing past me on all sides like hot gusts, brushing against me.

And I wasn't going to Princes Street, with its shops full of new coats and shoes. I was going the other way, out of the back of the station, up the steep hill, up the dark steps. On my lonesome.

Only, I wasn't alone. Those steps that climbed the side of the castle rock to the old town had deep doorways and overhangs, shady places where people with nowhere to go could pass this hot afternoon, drowsily asking for change, rousing themselves to shout at folk too posh or too mean to drop a coin, cackling at me, to be sure, for the way I squirted past them, eyes wide and heart banging.

'What do you think's going to happen to me?' I'd asked

my mum, while I was wheedling. 'What's going to happen to me in a *library*?'

At the top of the steps, I stopped to take the tenner out of my shoe. I'd got the idea from a story in a book but my sweaty bare foot in my old gutties had wadded it up, a ball under my instep, and I'd get a blister if I walked on it anymore. I shook it out, holding it by one corner, then poked it into my back jeans pocket, trying not to touch it too much, in case I squeezed actual droplets of foot sweat onto my fingers.

I could practically see the library from here. Just one big road to cross, one smaller one, and then all the beloved bulk of it loomed up beside me. I grabbed a railing to take the turn in through the gates as if the library was my dancing partner and we were doing a reel. My bag swung wide, away from my shoulder, and my hair lifted high, away from my neck, for one fresh moment. Then they both fell back, warm and thick against me.

I stared. I didn't even know the library had wooden doors. I'd never noticed them when they were thrown wide to either side of the entrance way. I'd only ever seen the glass doors before, smeared with fingerprints and blinded with signs, their brass handles glittering as if the same hands that dulled the glass somehow polished the metal.

'Shuts at one on a Saturday,' said a voice behind me. I turned. The man was smiling. His face was red and shone as his smile broadened. 'The National's still open,' he said, pointing across the road. 'Have you got a membership? For the National?' I shook my head. 'Not a problem,' he said, beaming now. I could see the inside bits of his cheeks bulging against his teeth. 'You can come in on mine.'

'That's very kind of you,' I began.

'Oh, I'm full of the milk of human kindness, me,' he

said. 'Full cream milk.'

I took a step. If we were crossing the road to the other library, he would have to turn and move that way but, as I took a second step, he was still standing square on, facing me.

'Tell you what, in fact,' he said. 'Seeing it's so warm today, why don't you and me step in somewhere first for a small refreshment? Plenty time for libraries later. When the sun goes down.'

I nodded. Behind him, only a foot behind him, people were passing in both directions, and two feet beyond *them* buses and cars groaned along, slowing for the lights, or picking up speed as they lumbered away. No one looked towards me. No one looks at the locked doors of a closed library.

'Thank you,' I said, but I didn't take a third step. 'It's so hot.'

'Too hot for jeans,' he said. 'You should have a nice wee sundress on. I could take you shopping, after we've had a drink or two.'

'A dress would be cooler,' I said and I managed to stretch my lips at him. He didn't see the smile for what it was. He wasn't really looking. What he did do, finally, was step to the side, opening one hand out to show the way and crooking the other elbow as if I might take his arm.

I smiled at him one last time then went up on the balls of my feet and ran. I ran like Sports Day, like the ice cream van was leaving, like I'd never run before.

He made a grab and managed to touch me. I felt his hot fingers through my sleeve but only the tips, uselessly dabbing at me, not nearly stopping me. And he didn't follow.

The red man was on at the big crossing and, safe inside a

nest of tourists, at last I looked back. He was watching but he was standing still and, as the green man came on and I was washed across to the far side, he grew smaller and smaller and I was away.

I went round the long road back to the station, zig-zagging down with the tourists, far from those steps and the jeers of the people taking the shade in the doorways. Then, back on the concourse, I stood and stared.

This was different from the station with its two platforms and a footbridge. I couldn't find the name of my home town anywhere on that giant departure board. Every time I was halfway through some list of destinations, a train would leave and everything would shift up, clacking over and resettling, so I couldn't tell what I'd read and what was new. So I started over. Then half a minute later, it happened again.

I could ask someone. I looked around for a British Rail uniform but all I could see was shoppers trudging and scowling, tourists pointing and gawping, teenagers older than me smirking and flirting, and all of them sweating, not a one of them noticing. Surely, though, someone would be kind enough, if I actually asked, to- *full of the milk of human kindness*. I heard it again, his voice even thicker in the remembering. Gluey, as if his throat was plugged with a bubble of spit.

So I went back to the platform I'd come in on, thinking that was probably right. Maybe it was even the same train sitting there, still filling.

It didn't look like the same train. This one had white cloth covers over the headrests and blinds on the windows. I slid into a seat and let my bag drop down between my feet, feeling the damp patch on my back where it had been resting. I'd never seen a train so empty. Only one person – a man in a suit, even though it was Saturday – came on and sat three rows ahead, frowning at me as he turned to stow his briefcase overhead.

I picked my bag up again. If it was still just him and me in here when the train moved off I'd go through to another compartment. I hated stepping over those connectors between the carriages when the train was moving. But if it was still just him and me, I'd go.

I was watching out for more people coming to join us and so I didn't notice the next man arriving. The first I knew was it got darker from him standing by my seat, stopping the light reflecting in the window. I turned, feeling my breath catch and my pulse do something it had never done before, as if it was frilled instead of plain now.

But it was the ticket collector and I breathed out again.

'This your seat?' he said. He was smiling, but not with all of his face. His lips were turned back to show his teeth but his eyes weren't squeezed up like smiling makes eyes usually. And he looked enormous, looming over me, because I was even smaller than I should have been, from the way I was scooted down, balanced on my shoulder blades to lift my bum off the seat and dig in my back pocket for the return bit of my ticket. I handed it up to him, noticing how the ink had smudged. His hand was damp too and he smudged it worse.

'Didn't think so,' he said. 'I saw you get on. You didn't strike me as a first-class ticket-holder.'

'I'll move,' I said. 'Sorry.'

'Oh you will, will you?' said the ticket man. 'That's big of you!'

'What?' I said.

'You're coming with me to Security, Little Miss Innocence.'

'I made a mistake.'

'Blagging onto a London train with a day-return runabout ticket?' he said. 'No kidding.'

'*London?*' I was on my feet. 'I can't go to London.'

'Not on this,' he said, waving my ticket at me. He let me squeeze by him and then poked me between my shoulders. 'Start walking. I'm right behind you.'

I passed the man in the suit. He was kidding on he wasn't listening, but I caught his eye in the window at his side. And that wasn't all I caught. I caught the reflection of all the empty seats I was passing too. Red upholstery, white headrests, bare tables. The ticket man wasn't behind me.

I looked over my shoulder. He was still at my seat, bending down, stretching towards the floor.

I ran. I was out of the train, off the platform, across the concourse and deep in a crowd, before I took a breath. Or so it felt like anyway, from the way I had to heave in chestful after chestful when I stopped moving, gulping down the reeking station air until my head swam and my vision fizzed with dark sparkles. I sank down against the deep sill of a boarded-up window, thick with grime and crusted with pigeon dirt.

He still had my ticket clutched in that sweaty hand. And I couldn't buy another one because I knew why he was bending down. I knew what he was reaching for. I'd pulled the crumpled tenner out of my back pocket along with my ticket, hadn't I? I didn't even need to check. I knew.

'You okay?'

This one wasn't even smiling. Wasn't even pretending to.

I ran.

Then I saw her. Mrs Something. She worked at the different hairdressers from where my mum got her hair done, and she went to the different pub from where my dad stopped in after his evening class, but she was from my town and she was headed home.

They were all headed home, shoving onto a train already full, every seat taken. I darted in ahead of a woman so heavy and hot and laden with carrier bags she couldn't be bothered to stop me. I threaded along the carriage; a smoking carriage, fugged and dim with it. I ignored the tutting as I elbowed through, squirming past bodies packed too tight to get out of my way. I planted myself halfway between the two doors, a fat man behind me and a fat woman in front of me. I was invisible. And even if I wasn't, there was no way a ticket man could get through this crowd to check them. I was safe, crammed in here with a hundred knackered, sweating, smoking women.

I looked around them all. Hair flat instead of curled, frizzed instead of flat, bag straps cutting into bare shoulders leaving weals like whip marks on sunburned skin, ankles puffed and armpits darkening, they surrounded me. The smell of their smoke, the early morning perfume they'd put on, the late afternoon BO, their blistering feet slipped out of their sandals and steaming, they engulfed me.

As we rocked away out of the station, I thought it was just the crush of us all. When we stopped in the tunnel, to groans all round, I eased aside to make some room. But there it was again. One of my buttocks was warmer than the other. There was a hand cupping it, squeezing it. Under cover of the crowd, someone with great big hands – both hands now, both bum cheeks – was kneading me through my jeans in time with the beat of the idling engine.

'No!' I said, sharp enough that every woman in the carriage looked up at me. The one standing right in front craned to stare, her eyes round inside the rings of her wrecked mascara. 'Get your filthy hands off my arse,' I said, loud like my drama teacher always told me, from right down inside me all the way out to the back wall. The warmth faded as he snatched his hands away.

'You wish!' He tried for scorn but his voice trembled.

'What makes you think I'm talking to you, Genius?' I said, trying for scorn and hitting a bullseye.

The women nearest us were tittering now.

'I wouldn't touch your arse if you paid me!' He sounded more sure of himself. Maybe he thought they were laughing with him, at me.

'Oh, yeah, that's right!' I said. One of the women winked at me. 'Girls are always looking for trouble out of a clear blue sky.' Another woman gave me a thumbs up. 'We're known for it.' Four teenaged girls sitting round a table started slow clapping.

'Your word against mine, doll,' he said.

'Not necessarily,' I said. I took another look up the length of the carriage, catching every eye. No one looked away. No one looked down. No one blinked.

'Let's vote on it,' I said. 'Let's see.'

About Catriona McPherson

Catriona was born in Scotland and lived there until 2010, before immigrating to California. A former academic linguist, she is now a full-time fiction writer, the multi-award-winning and best-selling author of the Dandy Gilver detective stories, set in Scotland in the 1920s. She also writes a strand of award-winning contemporary standalone novels including Edgar® finalist *The Day She Died* and Mary Higgins Clark finalists *The Child Garden* and *Quiet Neighbors*. Catriona was the Toastmaster for Malice Domestic 30 (2018).

To find out more about Catriona McPherson, visit http://catrionamcpherson.com/.